A
Mighty Word

A Mighty Word.

A Novel

Joshua Rex

ROTARY

ROTARY

PRESS

A MIGHTY WORD

©2021 by Joshua Rex
All Rights Reserved

ISBN: 9781735454115

Copyedited by S. T. Joshi

Cover Image from publicdomainpictures.net
(by Karen Arnold)

Additional Cover Work and Editing by
Joshua Rex

Rotary Press logo by Gian Romagnoli

FOR

Mary Jeanne Weyer

APRIL 12TH, 1921 – MARCH 25TH, 1989

PROLOGUE

They woke to a world that had forgotten them.

They didn't know why they'd come back, out of their mausoleums and up from the ground, emerging in a new century like animated time capsules. Yet there they were, risen and somehow sustained, though they drew no breath and though no hearts pounded within their barren interiors.

They felt no pain, no warmth when the sun shone like a re-imagined idol, nor chill when the moon rose through the unnatural glow of electric light tainting the night firmament. Smell and taste had not rejoined them, but they could hear the bewildering cacophony all around. It was visceral noise: the grinding alien racket and intentional dissonance, the drone of flying things, and the relentless hiss of wheeled machines speeding by. They saw, too. From behind the iron pike bars enclosing their necropolis, they huddled in their tatters, silently observing with unmitigated awe the star-studded beacons and towers in the distance, and the hard angles and blank, artless façades of the houses surrounding them.

Most frightful of all were the coarse people, carelessly dressed and slipshod of tongue. The furtive dead hid in their tombs when these contemporary philistines passed by the gates and tromped through the grounds, throwing trash and casually defacing the monuments. The more the dead regarded them, the more they realized how much time had passed; just how long they'd been Gone.

They met in the above-ground vaults, first choosing to remain concealed within the cemetery, then electing one or two individuals to venture outside the grounds. This had been decided after much debate. It had been the Reverend Edward Vanquit, still robed in his rotted vestments, reciting a line from a favorite hymn of their times, "Why should we start, and fear to die? What timorous worms we mortals are . . ." *that decided the matter. Not that they were any longer mortal, as it were, nor did they pretend to claim (save for the reverend himself) any allegiance to the religion they'd once upheld as their guarantee of eternal life. They had re-emerged in this uncharted age, stripped not only of their flesh, but the promise of salvation. Those chosen to wander the unfamiliar streets in their brittle bonnets or coattails clotted with mool returned with shocking details of astounding achievements amidst cultural deterioration; of wondrous technological advances diluted by decadence; of unspeakable lasciviousness and reckless disposability.*

And what about they, the forgotten? Had anything remained of their epoch or influence? Hardly. This age had all but erased and dismantled them, relegated their accomplishments to the realms of quaintness and antiquity. Despite this, the vast consensus sought contact—a link to the present through which they might come to understand these moderns, with all their inscrutable proclivities and paradoxes. Gradually, those who had built the city, and for over a century and a half lay buried beneath it, would emerge, make themselves Known. They would remonstrate with the Living, who thought they could be rid of the past simply by burying it. History was indeed a fragile thing, but truth—immutable.

They would remind them.

I.

"Our dead are never dead to us until we have forgotten them: they can be injured by us, they can be wounded; they know all our penitence, all our aching sense that their place is empty, all the kisses we bestow on the smallest relic of their presence."

GEORGE ELIOT
Adam Bede

"I have imbibed the shadows of fallen columns . . . until my very soul has become a ruin."

EDGAR ALLAN POE
MS. Found in a Bottle

1

Kevin Heartstone walked the cracked sidewalks beneath the rusting plane trees, relishing the warm wind of a seemingly unending Indian summer. Kevin's mother hated that he went on these midnight jaunts—in fact, forbade him from taking them. But she went to bed much earlier than he, and though he knew she hardly slept, she never emerged from her room until her 6 A.M. work alarm sounded. It was true that his community wasn't the safest in the city, but it wasn't as rough as Shadywood or Buckeye Heights, where the sound of gunshots was as common as firecrackers in early July. But neither was it Royalsburg, the new and affluent suburb on the west side where the higher-ups from Preventative Solutions were building their gated estates. Dovetree, one of the oldest neighborhoods in the city, was approaching its biennial. Its blocks were populated mostly with rundown four-square and gable-front National style houses—post-railroad era constructions built for the employees of the once prosperous steel mill, now a scab-colored hulk barely maintaining a pulse of productivity in the valley below.

There were plenty of dangers; assaults, larceny, murders—all of which were on the decline, yet occurring with enough regularity to keep the suburbanites' visits brief, and then only to the trendy restaurants and boutiques occupying the previously derelict buildings in the small downtown. Regardless of the risks, Kevin *had* to walk (he carried a pocket knife—one engraved with his initials, which his father had given him on his eleventh birthday). Not only did it keep the grief from pooling blackly in his sedentary limbs, but the aesthetic of the historic homes and buildings filled him with a sense of familiarity and love that were the antidotes for both his seemingly interminable despair and instinctive unease with modern life.

He had a route, one developed unconsciously night after night over the last few years, until it had become so fixed in his mind he could traverse it without looking up. It began at a set of wooden stairs that led down the hill next to his house—a rambling Queen Anne in which he and his mother lived on West 9th Street on the neighborhood's south side. The house perched on a rise overlooking Interstate 31, the highway that cleaved Dovetree into two sections. A footbridge connected the halves, beginning practically in Kevin's backyard, continuing over the interstate, and emptying onto the north side of West 9th, which ran along the edge of Garfield Park and terminated at a bluff that overlooked the city skyline. For Kevin, this was a sacred passage, one he'd walked countless times with his father, down the staggered steps to the mouth of the bridge, then on to Groft Mini Grocery or the Dovetree branch of the Still City public library, or grimy Sal's Pies where Kevin would play pop-ball or the 16-bit racing game with the worn buttons and wonky joystick while his father paid for their pizza. On their way to and from, Kevin would gaze up at the old, silent houses, intrigued by their intricate details, the names for which his father would provide. Thus at an early age, Kevin learned the parlance of his father's trade: lintel and quoin, cornice and cresting, finial and frieze. He learned the difference between Tudor and ogee arches, the order of Roman columns and the anatomy of their capitals and bases.

From this admiration of the craftsmanship of the past came a burgeoning fascination with the people who had built and once lived within these structures. While his father assessed plans for historic restorations at the antique architect's desk in his study, Kevin would perch on the rose-colored vintage sofa beside the fireplace with a pile of old books, studying the clothing and furniture and design of the nineteenth century. One of his favorites was a contemporary publication of restored early photographs: daguerreotypes, ambrotypes, tintypes, et al. For hours he would gaze at those long-disintegrated faces. The longer he stared, the more they seemed to speak to him. As this solemn communion deepened, Kevin felt increasingly cut off from the world tethered to a three-pronged electrical cord—an estrangement that redoubled four years ago when a man texting while driving ran Frank Heartstone's pickup into a bridge abutment just yards from the footbridge near Kevin's house.

Kevin had three clear memories from the funeral: the slightly buzzing tone of his paternal grandmother's incessant weeping; the way the funeral parlor lights picked up particles of windshield glass in his father's hair that the embalmer had somehow missed; and most lucidly, glimpsed on his way out the door, the funeral director closing the coffin lid—hastily, without any of the false reverence he'd displayed during the wake.

And ever since, Kevin had felt things closing within himself, just at the moment when the thrilling, enigmatic machinery of adolescence had begun revving up. The Present met a stone door in him, one belonging to a sealed tomb in which the only light came from memory.

His reverence for the Past was like a religion, an obsession that isolated him the more devoted he became. Since the dead offered no dialogue, he sought their voices in their literature and art and buildings, and was himself gutted when one of those old places was stripped, remodeled, or met the wrecking ball. During his walks, he would search the newly vacant lots for scraps of the recently demolished, finding perhaps a plaster acanthus curl from a Corinthian column, a spandrel or bracket dowel, a pane from a latticed window. On one of the sites he'd almost gotten caught climbing into an industrial rent-a-dumpster for a corbel. There he'd squatted amidst that sacred wreckage as a police spotlight scanned the area for what seemed like an eternity before finally moving on.

Tonight, however, he was not scouring any lots or dumpsters, only making his way through the fog. Pale green and with the stringent stink of burnt plastic, it rolled in nightly from north, spreading out over Dovetree and the adjacent neighborhoods like a funerary shroud. Everyone knew its source, but no one spoke of it. The media were equally as silent, their reticence fueled not only in the interest of sustaining the recent boost to the local economy, but (as they told themselves) for the good of the city, for it had to be said, where would they be without the daily reassurance of Plaiscene? The fog was an unfortunate by-product, but with ten thousand new weekly diagnoses nationwide, along with the tens of millions already consuming the little emerald pill daily, the smokestacks of Preventative Solutions showed no signs of slowing.

Kevin himself did not take Plaiscene, although it had been recommended by both the PS drug recruit representative who'd done a presentation at Kevin's school and by Jenna Heartstone, who had helped to engineer it. She was certain it would cure her son's depression, despite the fact that it hadn't alleviated her own. These days it seemed everyone was searching for guarantees and easy answers, Kevin thought. He had read about the helplessness of previous generations in the face of cholera and dysentery and typhoid and consumption, each with the power to erase entire families in mere days. To the contemporary mindset this was unthinkable. It was, mercifully, one of the appalling aspects of the past that had been left safely behind in antiquity. For the silver and black faces on tin and glass, Death had been There at all times; an inexorable, shape-changing phantom in their communities. If there was one consolation in having to endure the great droning indifference of the twenty-first century, it was that Death—in the way it had been for the Victorians—was for the most part on the perimeter of modern daily life.

But this proved to be just another contemporary chimera when his father was crushed against a bridge, and Kevin understood that Death was not remote, but sitting right beside him always, intimate as his own thoughts. There were no certainties, no escape from pain—not even in the form of Plaiscene.

He was brooding over this yet again as he treaded along the northernmost aspect of Dovetree—the bluff with

14

the view of downtown. The limey mist festooned the tops of the skyscrapers like seaweed on a shipwreck and hovered eerily over the long bands of meandering highway spanning the obscured waterway below. Far off in the east, where the Kiksuyapi River emptied into Lake Ahkohton, the lights of the Preventative Solutions complex pulsated, illuminating the plant with its funnels billowing green clouds and the sleek black shard-shaped headquarters building. Kevin headed down West 5th Street, passing his old elementary school and the newly rebuilt housing project, turned onto Plymouth Avenue, which ran through town center, and continued on south toward the park and home. The neighborhood wasn't without its great houses; they were dotted throughout, though mostly around the outskirts of the park, where they stood in varying states of decay, hedged in behind barriers of twisted chain-link fence. The majority was beyond any logical financial restoration commitment, yet they were being bought up nonetheless, the investors hoping that as the locality "gentrified," as the papers claimed it was doing, the values would return. This was a long way off by anyone's estimation. For the time being, Dovetree remained, in effect, an architectural graveyard.

It was in the weedy driveway of one of these ruins that Kevin saw the face peering at him through the fog. At first he thought it was one of the tatterdemalion drug addicts who loitered at the ends of the highway exit ramps holding crumpled sections of cardboard with messages like "Please Help God Bless" scrawled on them in marker. He'd heard they squatted in these houses, pissing on the parquet floors and smashing beer cans into the lincrusta. Kevin's heart began to race. He fingered the engraved initials *FH* on the knife handle, hearing his mother's voice in his mind: *"It's very selfish of you to go out walking at night like that. I wouldn't survive your funeral too, Kevin. I barely did your father's . . ."*

For a long time he and the figure stood staring at each other through the fog. Then, slowly, it began to shift, and Kevin saw the man's face. It was haggard, though not creased and sun-baked like those of the junkies. This visage was shriveled and cracked, the few remaining teeth jutting from ossified gums. Too gray, too gaunt, too *still*. Mutton chop sideburns clung to his cheeks like thatches of cobweb. He wore a black overcoat, a neatly tied cravat, and a top hat. Most unnerving were the man's eyes, burning a brighter green through the already green mist as they considered Kevin. The man looked up at the ruin's rickety fire escape, glanced back at Kevin, then suddenly took off across the street and ran into the park.

Kevin chased after him, past the lampposts and vacant benches. The man reached the gazebo at the center of the park, leapt through it but tripped on the stair coming out and, flailing, landed hard on the sidewalk. It was a bad fall—broken bones bad—yet the man got to his feet and immediately started sprinting in the direction of West 9th Street and the footbridge. It made Kevin pause. *What the hell?* By the time Kevin reached the bridge, the man was halfway across. A blast of wind from a passing semi on the highway below knocked the hat off his head. Kevin snatched it up mid-stride. The man didn't look back; when he reached the other side, he dashed into a patch of shallow woods left of the path and disappeared.

Kevin stood under the single flickering sodium arc light at the end of the bridge, examining the hat as he caught his breath. It was vintage—of that there was no doubt—made of hatter's plush and accented with a wide band of dark gray silk around the crown. The thing was dirty and musty and smelled sulphury. The lining was stained and brittle and flaked under his fingers. Sewn into this was a tag with a name: "W. M. Gladden." The streetlight suddenly burned out and Kevin went cold, standing there alone with the hat in his hands.

He hurried up the hill to his house, slid his key in the lock, and went in. The silence on the other side of the door seemed solemn and unnerving. After four years, he still wasn't used to it. Kevin crept up to his room; the stairs were old, but he knew just where to step to keep them from creaking.

His room was austere and decidedly curious for a fifteen-year-old. No rock band posters, no sports pennants, no digital alarm. A narrow sleigh bed stood in one corner under the room's north-facing window. There was a Gothic Revival chair topped with a spiral finial in the corner opposite of the bed, and beside it a little side table with a pewter candle stick and half-burned taper. To the right of this was a bow-front chest of drawers, the top crowded with old family pictures in antique frames. In the drawers and in his closet were white T-shirts, jeans, plain button-down long-sleeve shirts. A spring coat and a battered winter coat. One pair of sneakers and all-weather boots. Lastly, one of his father's work-worn hooded sweatshirts, which was too big for Kevin though he wore it often nevertheless. At the heart of the room was the secretariat desk, standing against the other window whose eastward view was obscured by a massive magnolia tree. Hanging from the desk chair was a canvas bag containing a hard-backed company ledger he used as a commonplace book, scrawling notes and drawings and lists within. Flanking the desk were the floor-to-ceiling bookshelves his father had built for him while renovating the house. Contained on these shelves was the center of Kevin's life: his personal library.

Kevin placed the top hat on the desk, lit a candle, and carried it to the shelves where he began scanning the spines for volumes on period costume. He drew out three books and perched on the edge of the desk chair, paging through the old tomes until he came to a section on nineteenth-century headgear. Comparing the photos to the artifact on his desk, he guessed it to be circa 1850. It confirmed his suspicion about the hat, but not its wearer. He picked it up again, read the name. Yes, he'd heard of W. M. Gladden; he'd seen it engraved somewhere. A cemetery? A plaque? Kevin considered it until he felt his eyelids begin to close. He put the hat back on the desk, blew out the candle, and went to bed.

But he didn't sleep. His gaze kept drifting back to the hat, a crouching shadow that seemed to look back at him. Suddenly he wished he'd left it on the bridge. It felt wrong that it was here, in his room with him. It wasn't its age; there were plenty of other old objects here. It was its appearance, its smell, its . . . *presence.*

Even when he turned over in bed, facing the window and the bone-white light of the tumescent moon, he swore he could feel it watching him.

2

Earlier that summer Mia Noblecourt, a film student at Still City State University, made a documentary about the city where she was earning her undergraduate degree. She was from a small town situated beside a national forest in the mountains of the northwest; a spacious, tranquil, meditative place, in decided contrast to the general gloom that the endless miles of vacant houses and shells of long-defunct industry here inspired. The focus of her work was the environmental legacy of a post-industrial urban area. On walks with her HDV camcorder and cell phone doubling as a Dictaphone, she would marvel at the massive brick ruins, built along the waterfront due to the ease of access for transportation, as well as waste dumping. For the most part this had been prevented by federal law over the last several decades, though there was a new factory, built at the crux of the lake and the river, that seemed to have been granted supra-legal status.

Though there were no visible pipes spewing toxic runoff from the Preventative Solutions manufacturing center, Mia knew through her research that the company was responsible for the raw green sludge hugging the coastline like a discarded Christmas garland. The papers called these "algae blooms," but who had ever seen algae that glowed, faintly neon, in the dark? Her interviews with local

18

commercial fisherman had provided her with images of mutated fish dredged up in their nets. Though they showed these to Mia and even let her photograph them, the men declined to comment and quickly tossed the aberrations overboard as soon as she left.

It wasn't only the water that was yielding disturbing phenomena. The pale green miasma that seeped up from the mud at the delta of the Kiksuyapi had been seen in other areas of Still City, particularly east in Uptown—a part of the city comprised mostly of vehicle impound lots, defunct shopping centers, housing projects, and a vast old graveyard. Mia discovered the highest concentration in and around Treestone Cemetery, where her covert infrared night-vision camera captured something much more disturbing than aberrant mist.

She took the footage to the *Lake-Times,* hoping to find some common journalistic ground on which to discuss her findings. She managed to secure a meeting with the deputy editor, who reprimanded her on slander and then delivered a not-so-veiled threat regarding the editor's professional and personal relationship with the head of the film department of SCSU before showing Mia the door.

But Mia wasn't deterred. Certain that she had entered serious conspiracy territory, the very next day, in a moment of undergraduate temerity, she put in an application at Preventative Solutions and was actually hired a week later as a "sanitation specialist"—the company's corporate euphemism for janitor. For the entire single month of her employment there, before her sudden, unexplained termination, she secretly filmed both the processing facility and the interior of the headquarters building using a camera sewn into her uniform. What she discovered was not only PS's culpability and direct responsibility for the environmental anomalies, but the city government's collusion. Plecebala, a latent stimulant found in Plaiscene, was being dumped undiluted into the waterways. It was also being belched from the factory's funnels and thus disseminated by deposition, slowly collecting on houses and trees and lawns like fallout. After viewing her unintentional footage, Mia discovered plecebala had the power to transmute via osmosis. Though environmental agencies in nearby counties voiced concern, the city's official position on the matter remained: "The fog poses no significant threat to life or the general ecosystem."

Political claptrap of course, but also revealing that the bureaucratic entities seemed unaware of the severity of the situation. Perhaps the best thing to do was to gather her findings and leave the state—find a private prosecutor or meet with the EPA and leave it to them to begin building a federal case. This was no mere school project anymore, no call-to-action documentary: an entire region was on the brink of an ecological crisis. She knew there was enough evidence to inculpate PS, as well as many of Still City's elected officials. Only the mayor's office had shown any interest in her claims, actually emailing her back and agreeing to view the Treestone Cemetery footage, which she immediately had sent. But that had been a month ago, and despite her many follow-up emails, Mia had yet to hear a response.

During those interposing weeks, she had been followed. It began soon after her dismissal from PS. She'd see them watching her in coffee shops, at the library, from other desultory locations throughout Still City. It was always a different person, always glimpsed retreating in her periphery. She went to the campus police, then the regular police. Each exhorted her to buy some mace and "try not to walk anywhere alone."

On the last day of November, Mia steered her clunky little hatchback into the lot of her apartment complex, parked between a pair of identical dark gray SUVs, gathered her bag and her digital camera along with a sack of Thai takeout food, and started across the warm blacktop. It was nearly ten P.M., but the temperature remained a persistent 78 degrees, this after a record high of 85 earlier in the day. Her car had no air conditioner. She was sticky and headachy and ready for a glass of cold white wine and som tum salad in front of her apartment's rattling A/C unit. Juggling her stuff, she got her key ready as she climbed the stairs leading up the outside of the building. But when she reached the third-floor landing, she found that there was no need for it. The apartment door stood wide open. Mia had no doubt what she'd find as she stepped inside.

Wreckage. The glass double doors leading to a small balcony off the living room were spiderwebbed. Her was desk askew, and her computer, HDV camcorder, and all her physical files were gone. Shaking with both rage and fear, she grabbed a chair, stood it up beside her bare desk, then sat down in it and cried. It had occurred to her just yesterday that she should probably back up all her data online. But the documentary, like the semester, was almost done. It would take too long, too much time away from finishing the piece, which needed to be completed by mid-December finals. Now none of that mattered. It was gone, all of it, all except the cemetery clip she'd emailed the mayor. Ironically, this was the most damning evidence of all, though without her recordings from within PS it looked like nothing more than a scene from a bad student horror film.

Mia sat there and wept, not only for the loss of her work, but in relief that she hadn't been at home when they'd come. She realized now she'd never paused to consider how serious the game was she'd been playing. The narrative in her head had been "Ingénue film student topples evil Major Corporation, saves a city, becomes documentarian superstar." How naïve she'd been, how close to real danger . . .

A sound, somewhere in the apartment. Mia looked up, pawing at her tears. Yes, those were footsteps. She heard the front door shut. Terror flashed through her. She ran to the sliding door and pulled the handle. It was locked, the latch intentionally broken off. Mia wrenched at it harder, an hysterical sound rising in her throat as she heard the approaching footsteps crunching glass, and then smelled the faint stink of burnt plastic.

Serge Vexivus stood at the window of his office located at the point of the blade of PSHQ, gazing out at the pier and the pewter lake. In the distance, a squall was gathering above a distant chain of islands fixed on the horizon line like enemy ships. This was good. By the end of every two-week production cycle, the fog grew so thick it could no longer be moved by mere wind. It took a good thrasher of a storm to disperse, and that was exactly what appeared headed their way—a gale to clear the city and quiet the growing suspicions. Serge did not like answering questions, nor the tedious people who asked them. He liked Plaiscene even less. It was ghastly stuff, repulsive; the stink of it filled his office, seeped into his clothes, followed him home. The reason people took it repulsed him more. *He* did not require mental conditioning; he did not think small, but decisively. Because of this Serge was, at thirty-two, the youngest chief of production of all PS's forty-nine branches. He hadn't gotten where he was by reasoning with his rivals or verbally pacifying his subordinates.

Gaunt and rangy, with a cadaverous face (he'd cultivated a Vandyke to appear less corpse-like) and a personality equally as inflexible, he had achieved his position because of his indomitable nature as well as his innate ability to manipulate bureaucracy and elected leaders. Paramount in his mind always was Profit, and the freedom to attain it unmolested by law and regulation. Still City had been the ideal environment for this until the EPA insisted PS install a super filter (at the company's expense, of course) to strip the erratic compound plecebala from its processing water before it flowed on to the treatment facility. The filter cost a phenomenal sum to operate—an expense, like the machine itself, which PS was solely to incur. The mandate meant a huge cut in revenue.

Serge brooded for weeks of teeth-grinding contemplation until he came up with a plan to bypass it. He

assembled a handpicked crew to build his "diverter"—
essentially a pipe laid in a tunnel dug several yards below the
new filter. Although this was a highly classified branch-
specific operation, he offered no additional perks for being
selected for the mission, no pay increase, no change in title.
Fear was the incentive, and he had made it very clear what the
consequence would be if any of the chosen spoke of it to
anyone outside the selected circle: what came to be known as
"taking a green bath." In order to appease the inspectors, lake
water spiked with a ten percent mixture of runoff was passed
through the super-filter via hydraulic pressure. The viscous
sludge would settle in the mesh gills, demonstrating proof of
use, while the remaining unadulterated ninety percent would
be split: forty-five percent emptying into the Ahkohton, the
other half trucked to various abandoned and semi-abandoned
areas throughout the city.

Serge didn't tell his superiors about the plan; he
hadn't received any formal approval. When the higher-ups
learned of his modifications, they were at first furious he
hadn't sought their prior consent. Yet the grumblings
stopped when, at the end of the first quarter following the
diverter's installation, the Still City branch of Preventative
Solutions remained the only of the forty-nine not to report a
twelve percent loss. Serge did not intend this to change.

The squall was blackening, dragging long trails of
precipitation behind it like tentacles. He heard the first distant
groan of thunder as the intercom on his desk buzzed and a
chiming female voice said:

"Mr. Vexivus? It's the mayor."

Serge scratched at his little pointed beard, a grating
hiss in the hermetic silence of the office. "I thought I made it
clear that I am not taking any *calls* from the mayor's office."

A pause, then: "Yes sir, you did. But he's not on the
phone. He's . . . here."

Drawing a long, slow breath, Serge picked up the
receiver. "Kaitlyn?"

"Yes, sir?"

"Send the mayor up to my office. After that, gather your things and get out of my building, you stupid incompetent bitch."

He slammed the phone down. He wanted to pick it up and slam it again, over and over until it was a pile of shattered plastic and rainbow wires. Instead he dimmed the lights, turned down the air conditioning a few ticks, and then sat at his desk, waiting for Prise. For all the recent heat wave, the room was freezing. It was an intimidation tactic, but it was also the way that Serge liked it. One might say he had inherited his forefather's blood, tempered by the frigid winters of northeastern Europe whence his family had migrated to a more moderate climate in the post–Great War period. His paternal great-grandfather was even semi-famous for being one of only three men known to have survived Siberian exile as a soldier, showing up in his hometown three months after being presumed dead; a haggard, skeletal figure, skin leathery and crackled like birch bark. He would spend the next forty years planting and plowing turnip fields without most of his toes and the fingers of one hand. But Serge had inherited his ancestor's sangfroid in more than one way.

A few short raps on the door; the mayor entered without being beckoned, accompanied by a pair of big bodyguards. John Prise was short and square-shaped, his neck a thick plinth supporting a head reminiscent of a classical bust with its prominent nose and close-cropped curls. Serge wondered if Prise, fresh from re-election to a second term, fancied himself sporting a crown of laurel. PS had funded a covert attempt to fix the ballot, but the mayor had still defeated his opponent by more than twenty percentage points. The optimism on which he and his platform of urban renewal swept into office his first term hadn't lessened despite the city's perennially high crime rate and sluggish job growth. There was still much work to be done: Prise had stressed this outwardly and often, though it was no secret to the people of Still City, with its crumbling infrastructure and public schools annually turning out more prisoners than graduates, at the beginning of his first term.

He had gotten everyone's attention by declaring a city-wide state of emergency. Though it was hyperbole and politics, it had brought in a good deal more federal money to help kick-start revitalization. His first major civil project had been as emblematic as it was practical: the restoration of Link Tower, the former headquarters of the Central-Link Railroad Co. At the time of its construction in the late '20s, it had been the tallest building in the country. Despite its current ranking as third of the city's six skyscrapers, the tower remained an icon—a symbol of Still City's former greatness and once prominent national status. Public Television had filmed during the repairs and renovations and would be airing a documentary upon the tower's completion, at which time the mayor would also disclose the recent approval of funds for repairs on a number of the city's other National Registry buildings, as well as the rebuilding of the Interstate 31 bridges (recently and harrowingly deemed structurally unsound), and the repaving of a thousand roads in the greater city area.

Paradoxically, it was Prise himself who had negotiated the deal to bring Preventative Solutions to Still City—a move that had been both his greatest triumph and regret. The promise of low taxes and relaxed regulation made the arrangement equally as attractive to PS. The mayor wasn't thrilled with the nature of the industry that would become synonymous with his city, but John Prise was as much a pragmatist as he was an idealist. People needed incomes, sought security. Civic pride didn't pay the bills. So when he heard that PS was searching for a new Midwest production base, he didn't waste any time contacting the corporate offices. Admittedly, John knew it was more about the five thousand jobs this had created—and not his historical revitalization projects—that had won him another term.

Serge Vexivus knew it too, and had made it very clear in a recent *Lake-Times* interview where he publicly challenged the mayor to act on his threat of stopping production if pollution levels weren't curtailed. This periodical war went on for months, during which the mayor's approval rating dropped a point per week. With Prise's popularity plummeting, Serge supposed the little man had come seeking détente.

"I'll keep this brief, Mr. Vexivus, therefore we won't have to waste any time on unpleasantries."

"Oh? That isn't what I had anticipated, Mr. Mayor."

"Here's something else that you probably didn't anticipate." Prise opened his valise and took out an electronic tablet. He swiped the screen, tapped it, and handed it to Serge, who took it reluctantly.

A video was playing, filmed in infrared. The scene was a cemetery. Several small mausoleums cast in pale green light were visible, flanking a path which meandered off into darkness. A firefly drifted by the camera lens; there was the sound of a car passing on the road behind. Otherwise nothing moved. Serge's eyes ticked up impatiently at the mayor. When he looked down at the screen again, he saw the doors of one of the tombs opening and a face peering around it. Serge felt a chill that had nothing to do with temperature of his office. The face with its bright green eyes like a night animal's, scanned the area, hesitating momentarily on the camera. Then the figure darted—surprisingly quick—to another tomb.

"Exactly what am I looking at?"

"Evidence of your company's non-compliance with federal regulations," Prise said. "Rather disturbing evidence indeed."

"How casually you throw your allegations around," Serge said, tossing the tablet on his desk. "Given your recent disapproval numbers, you'd think it would be prudent not to threaten the only institution responsible for your re-election."

"I'm not here to argue politics," Prise said.

"No? Then why *have* you come? To show me videos of vagrants playing hide and seek in a graveyard?"

"They're not vagrants, Mr. Vexivus," the mayor said.

"Fine. Crackheads, coloreds, prostitutes, whatever you want to call them . . ."

One of the mayor's bodyguards, a black man with a chest broad as a suitcase, took an inadvertent step toward Serge, but Prise stopped him with a gesture of the hand. Serge ticked up his eyebrows at the guard, as if some small personal joke had passed between them.

"This was shot at Treestone Cemetery," the mayor continued calmly, "where groundskeepers have recently reported a mass breach of burial plots, *below* as well as above ground. You see, Serge, those aren't technically people walking around in that cemetery."

"'Technically'? What the hell are you talking about?"

"They're dead."

Serge drew a sharp, exasperated breath and let it out. "Dead," he repeated.

The mayor nodded gravely. "As you are well aware, Plaiscene contains high amounts of plecebala, a chemical that aids in the stabilization of the brain's amygdala by regulating the hypothalamus. In pill form it is stable, easily and safely absorbable by the body. But in its raw state its behavior is unpredictable, particularly when mixed with molecular hydrogen—a reaction that is further accelerated by oxygen, meaning that H_2O is an ideal courier. Allegedly, the excess plecebala is filtered out at your facility, yet high concentrations of it have been turning up in the waterways, Uptown, and the soil at this cemetery. Over the last five weeks there have been twenty-eight reported cases of severe lung and kidney issues—those patients being, by and large, children and the elderly, all of whom are residents of Uptown and the surrounding vicinity. We have come to the conclusion that the chemical is also responsible for the 'reactivation' in Treestone. Lastly, the graduate student who filmed the footage you've just watched has disappeared, and her apartment was found ransacked. Eyewitnesses claim to have seen a pair of dark gray SUVs without tags speeding out of the complex's parking lot the same night—vehicles that

27

bore a rather familiar two-letter acronym."

Serge smiled. "Let me see if I understand this. You're here to accuse me of poisoning children, kidnapping, and . . . zombie making?"

"The media haven't gotten wind of any of this yet, but it is imminent. Perhaps the story's breaking as we speak. You see, there have been sightings *outside* of the cemetery as well as inside. People are afraid and asking questions. The EPA has been contacted and is currently investigating the affected areas to determine the source of the contamination. The sick are being treated, though in many cases the damage appears to be irreversible. The missing girl's disappearance is in the hands of the SCPD. I'm confident that each of these instances will be traced back to a single origin, and that it will result in the likely shutdown of Preventative Solutions nationally."

Serge opened the center drawer of his desk, drew out a single sheet of paper, and slid it across the black polished surface toward Prise. The document was official in all the right ways: printed on cream-laid paper, the letterhead embossed in dark blue and red, both signature and gold seal hand-applied.

"This is an affidavit from the executive branch of the federal government ordering that Preventative Solutions maintain a continuously running operation," Serge said. "This mandate is amendable and terminable only by that office. So, as you can see, Mr. Prise, neither you nor your city has the *authority* to shut down this company. As for the public's reaction, I believe they'll find an alternative source to blame if their jobs depend on it."

"I don't care on whose authority you are acting. You've turned my city into a cesspool. You're poisoning my people. You're going to be held responsible for it."

"You like to call yourself a 'man of the people,' Mr. Prise. But like all liberals, your faith is misguided. *People*, John, are not good. They want only for themselves, and they are willing to follow any course that might ensure their own

28

comfort and security."

"You are describing yourself, not the citizens of this city," Prise said.

Serge knitted his long, bony fingers and leaned forward on his desk. "I'm sure you're aware that six out of every ten individuals in this city currently take Plaiscene every day. Do you have any idea *why* they've been prescribed it? It's not because they're confident and industrious and beaming with pride at being valued members of their community. They're frightened, broken, lonely people without direction or hope. They are also lazy and stupid and need to be told what to do and what to buy and what is best for them."

"And you take pride in exploiting these insecurities. Or perhaps your objective is to *create* them?"

"I am not the enemy, merely a facilitator. Denying people what they need is not the best way of securing a political future. They *need* Plaiscene," Serge said, though as he looked at Prise, it was clear that the mayor himself wasn't among them. The guards were, however; their lips had darkened, and the whites of their eyes had glazed with that tell-tale faint shade of olive green.

The mayor stood. "I am going to do everything in my power to expose you, your product, and the nightmare you've created, regardless of *my* political future. I suggest *you* prepare for the forthcoming mass dissent."

The stink of the mayor's cologne hung in the air after he'd left. Serge returned the sheet of paper to the desk drawer, then picked up the phone and pressed two numbers. Someone answered, though they did not speak. Serge instructions were brief. Afterwards, he gently hung up the receiver and returned to the window.

Wind and rain buffeted the darkened glass. In the distance he saw a pair of gulls hovering around the end of the break wall where another had pulled a fish out of the water. Its sleek silvery body writhed and slapped against the rough-hewn stone as the fisher bird pecked at its eyes. The others swooped down through the greenish haze and began picking at its flesh.

Serge watched them until there was nothing left of the fish but a latticework of bone.

4

Life in the Still City Municipal school district, where more funding went to security than education technology, was treacherous, and Clinton High School was no exception. Drug infestation, exhausted teachers, and a scarcity of tax money resulted in an atmosphere in which survival often took precedence over learning. Kevin, who had spent his entire life in the system, had learned long ago that in order to survive one must remain in the periphery at all times, as invisible as possible.

For Kevin—five foot seven and slightly built—this wasn't difficult. He dressed plainly and had plain features: sandy hair (which darkened a little more each year), hazel eyes, and a pallor that testified to his time spent indoors. But in this atmosphere, even answering questions in class could be parlous (in fourth grade, a classmate had given him a black eye for correctly naming all seven continents). So Kevin remained silent most of the time, responding only in order to maintain a participation grade.

Despite his reticence, he excelled in his studies, diligently following the lessons and supplementing his learning with private study. And despite the district's poverty, rampant crime, narcotics plague, and his school's overall abysmal performance rating, he found that the potential to rise above it all was right there, lain before him—all he had to do was put the work in. Kevin, along with a handful of his classmates ("Tryers" he called them—it wasn't the most interesting nickname, but it accurately described them), did just this. He was cordial with the other Tryers, though he didn't necessarily consider any of them friends.

Besides the unseasonable warmth, the last day of November was just an average Friday, with classes half full and the hour hand creeping around the clock. Kevin sat in his seventh-period Historical Fundamentals class, gazing out the barred windows in a rare moment of daydream. He couldn't stop thinking about the hat and its mysterious owner. Kevin didn't believe in ghosts, yet there had been something ghostly about the figure, or anachronistic at the very least. What had he been doing lurking around that ramshackle house? Had he lived there before? Grown up there? As Kevin thought about the man's clothes, his overall appearance, the unusual litheness of his movements, a tantalizing yet totally absurd idea began to coalesce in his mind—at exactly the same moment he became aware of Ms. Balconet repeating his name over and over again.

"Kevin *Heartstone*."

Ripped from his reverie, Kevin turned to find the entire class looking at him. No longer invisible, Kevin felt a spike of terror drive into his chest like a stake.

"Why was the Reconstruction period of the post–Civil War era a failure for the recently freed slaves?"

He knew the answer, but with all those eyes on him all he could do was stammer. After a few agonizing seconds, Ms. Balconet's gaze drifted over his head. "Yes?" she said.

"Because the northern states gradually abandoned their cause," a female voice behind Kevin said, "leaving them at the mercy of the southern state governments. Programs to aid with the integration of freed blacks into one national society were discontinued, and the new citizens were left to fend for themselves."

"That is correct. Despite the ratification of the Thirteenth, Fourteenth, and Fifteenth Amendments, the South found ways to circumvent integration. This is one of the primary reasons that the legacy of slavery continues to this day . . ."

Kevin looked over his shoulder. He didn't recognize the girl, though this wasn't uncommon in a graduating class of close to 1500. Still, she was a Tryer, and he thought he knew all the Tryers. Her skin was coffee with cream, her kinked hair long, lips full and shell pink. He found himself unable to look away from her lapidary blue eyes. She raised her eyebrows, and Kevin, realizing he was staring, turned quickly back around in his seat. He was oblivious to the rest of the lesson, consumed by a growing, uncharacteristic urge to talk to the girl. When the bell sounded the end of the period, Kevin turned again and said:

"Thanks for saving me on that. I kind of froze up."

The girl was stuffing her books into her backpack, pretending not to hear him.

"It was a good answer," he said.

"It's not the whole answer," she muttered without looking up.

"What do you mean?"

She looked him up and down. "*You* wouldn't understand."

The girl slid out of her seat, looped the backpack over her shoulder, and walked out, leaving Kevin alone in the classroom where the weekend silence had already begun to settle over the empty desks like dust.

5

Kevin had been dreading this particular Friday for one all-pervading reason: it was the day he was finally going to meet *Chaz*.

His mother had been talking about the guy for the last month, casually dropping his name into their conversations as the weeks progressed. On Wednesday she'd asked if Kevin would mind if this Chaz came over for dinner. He'd lied, said he didn't, though in truth it infuriated him to think of another man entering his father's house—the same house they'd restored together as a family, the house that had become a posthumous shrine to Frank Heartstone's memory. That memory was sacred, of course; the threat to it had brought Kevin and his mother to yet another impasse, but this one neither knew how to negotiate.

Kevin got home first, grabbed a soda from the fridge and a bag of salt-and-vinegar chips from the cabinet, and shut himself in his room. He tossed his backpack in the closet, cracked open the can of fizzy orange drink, and immersed himself in a volume of cemetery folk art, turning pages in between handfuls of chips. Around six, his mother came home. She uttered a cautious hello as she passed his door. He said hello back, but there was no face-to-face time as usual. Kevin continued reading, noting a quotation from one of the headstones that he found appropriate: "The memory of the just is blessed." He copied it down in his journal/commonplace book under his notes about the top hat.

An hour passed. Kevin dozed, and woke to voices in the foyer: his mother's—higher and more excitable than usual, and another, lower one, foreign as unfamiliar cologne. Kevin put a pair of headphones on and played a record. A little while later the stink of cooked meat trailed in under his door. Kevin had gone vegetarian after his father died, so the smell made him nauseous. He was stuffing a coat in the crack under his door when his mother suddenly knocked. Reluctantly he opened it for her and she came in, shutting the door behind her.

"Chaz is here. He made us dinner."

Kevin sat at his desk, picked up the top hat, and began turning it in his fingers.

"Where did you get that?" she asked.

"Found it."

"Where?"

"On the footbridge."

"You found *that* on the footbridge? Why was it—"

"I'll be right down, okay?"

Exasperation flashed in his mother's eyes, replaced by a grating look of resolute cheer. "Great, I'll let him know."

The reek of grilled fat and fried onions grew stronger as Kevin descended the stairs, disorienting and foreign. It had been four years of frozen dinners and restaurant takeout since his father (who usually did the cooking) had died. Three places had been set at the large gate-leg table: two on one side, and one across from them. Kevin couldn't recall the last time he and his mother had eaten here. The table itself had become merely a temporary repository for Jenna's work papers and Kevin's to-be-returned library books.

He sat on the side set for one, under the low light of the elaborate chandelier he'd helped his father clean and restore crystal by crystal. He looked at the two plates, two forks, two knives, two glasses across from him. Frank's seat at the head of the table was vacant. Kevin could easily picture him there, dressed in one of those faded work flannels he'd worn invariably both at the design desk and the work site, his prematurely silver hair contrasting with a tanned and mostly unlined face.

Beyond the double doors that led to the kitchen Kevin could hear his mother's furtive whispers interspersed with that alien baritone. He looked away from his father's empty chair, swiping at a tear. A minute later the doors swung open and his mother and a balding, paunchy late thirty-something with small stony eyes entered the dining room. Each held a large glass of red wine; the presumed Chaz's other hand was on Jenna Heartstone's backside. She slapped it away and straightened her skirt. Kevin could tell by her rutilant cheeks that she'd already had a few Cabernets.

"So this is the amazing Kevin I've heard so much about," Chaz said. He held out a hand and Kevin, half rising from his seat, shook it. Chaz's fingers were small and thick, his grip firm.

"Nice to meet you," Kevin said in a voice that didn't sound his own.

"I hope you're hungry," Chaz chuckled, glancing at Jenna. "We made a ree-*diculous* amount of food."

Kevin forced a smile.

"Why don't you two sit down and I'll dish it up," Chaz said.

"Don't you need some help?" Jenna asked.

"Nah, I got it," Chaz said as he gathered the plates and disappeared back into the kitchen.

"You're using the special dishes," Kevin said. He picked up the antique fork from his place setting and turned it in his fingers, gloomily regarding the curling "H" monogram stamped on the handle. Frank had inherited the flatware from his great-grandmother.

"It's a special occasion," his mother answered.

Kevin looked up. "Is it?"

"Chaz has been looking forward to meeting you."

Kevin set the fork down. Jenna took a deep drink of wine. "How was school?"

"Fine. How was work?"

"All right. The mayor came in today."

"Did you ask him why he never comes over anymore?"

Frank Heartstone and John Prise had been roommates in college and good friends until Frank's death. He had assumed a sort of avuncular role in Kevin's life, but Kevin had only seen John a few times since the funeral—most likely because it had coincided with the beginning of Prise's first term as mayor, though it was still not an excuse.

"I think it makes him sad," Jenna said solemnly.

"Yeah," Kevin said softly.

Jenna set her wine glass on the table and leaned forward. "Kevin, I know this is strange. I'm not trying to pretend it isn't. It is for me too, believe it or not. Just *try* for me, will you? See how it goes?"

Chaz elbowed through the double doors, carrying in each hand a plate with a huge steak and a pile of battered fried onions. He set one down in front of Jenna, then Kevin. "One for the lady, and one for the big guy." Kevin gave his mother an incredulous look. Chaz popped back into the kitchen and returned with his own plate, which he set on the table, eyeing it proudly, feverishly. He cut a hunk from the rare T-bone, pale juice dripping on the antique table linen as the fork moved from the plate to Chaz's gaping maw. Beside him, Jenna picked up her knife and scraped the thick crust of salt and seasoning off the massive hunk of meat on her plate.

"Your mother tells me you like history," Chaz said as he chewed.

"Yeah."

"What kind?"

"You mean in general?"

Chaz shrugged. "Sure."

"Architectural. My *father* was an architect."

"Right, your mother told me," Chaz said while sawing along a band of gristle. "I work with old places too, you know."

"Where?"

"I'm a site manager for Resurrection Foundations."

"The *demolition* company?"

"Well, demolition's not all we do. Half of our focus is on new development in the community. We just wrapped up at the Dovetree Commons. Things are really starting to clean up in this neighborhood."

"You mean those ugly box condos that went up on the site of the Henry Nix house?"

Chaz frowned. "Henry Nix house . . ."

"You know, the Carpenter Gothic at 2888 Star Lane?"

"Wow, you *do* know your buildings!" Chaz said. "I bet it was really quaint and cozy in its day. You should have seen it inside. Disgusting. I don't think it had been touched since the eighteen-hundreds. Missing nine windows, roof collapsed, and there was a foot of *raw sewage* in the basement!"

Kevin had a flashback of standing before the Nix house with his father one winter afternoon. The flecked white paint on the weatherboard looked as fragile as the snowflakes falling around the place. "This city's returning to life," Frank had said, almost crooned. "One day soon someone's going to buy this place and give it the love it needs. And wait until you see it when they do, Kevin . . . that is, if they do it properly."

Kevin had looked up at his father, wishing he could

see inside his mind, at what Frank saw as he eyed the ruin, returned once again to its former magnificence: the gingerbread gable trusses repainted, the lancet panes replaced, the sagging porch with its decorative trellises re-secured. But that hadn't happened, because Chaz and Resurrection Foundations had mown it down and put an incongruent eyesore in its place. That was what "bringing back the city" meant to them.

"That property value's quadrupled. A good thing for you with this place, Jenna, when you—"

"Kevin, why aren't you eating?" Jenna broke in suddenly.

"I'm a vegetarian," Kevin said.

"No, you're *not*," Jenna scoffed.

"Yes I *am*," Kevin said. "You should know that by now."

Chaz's knife grated to a halt against his plate mid-cut. He looked from Kevin to Jenna and whispered: "I thought you said he liked steak."

"He does."

"No, I *don't*," Kevin said. He threw his cutlery on top of the bloody slab lying on his plate and pushed it hard across the table. It collided with Jenna's wine glass, knocking it over and sending a flood of cab-franc surging into her lap.

"*Dammit*, Kevin!"

"Here, I got it, Jen," Chaz said. He was up at once, righting the glass, attempting to sop up the wine with his bloodstained napkin. "Rags are in the upstairs closet, right?"

As Chaz dabbed futilely at the blotch of red blooming across the ruined linen, Kevin looked up slowly at his mother. It was the casual way Chaz had referred to her—"Jen"—and yes, even something as mundane as knowing where the rags were kept told Kevin: *He's been here before.* And not just once. Probably many times. She'd brought the demolition expert here—into their house, into her bed. She'd done it slyly, without asking Kevin or considering his feelings. As usual, she only cared about *herself,* *her* grief, *her* loneliness.

Kevin pushed back from the table and stomped out of the room and back upstairs. In his periphery he saw Chaz coming down the hall toward him with a threadbare towel. Kevin did not look at him as he entered his room and slammed the door. A few seconds later Jenna was there. She didn't bother knocking, just came in, shut the door, and stood in front of it.

"I know what you're thinking, and it's not true," she said.

"You mean you're *not* screwing that guy?"

"I *mean* that you think I don't still love your father."

"You're a liar," Kevin said, tears brimming. "You wouldn't have brought *him* here if you did!"

"Kevin, you have to understand something. Things happen in life—things that no one has any control over. They can happen to anyone at any time . . . to the people we love the most, and there's nothing we can do about it."

"Yeah, I think I've found that out, Mom."

"Someday you'll understand that adults need comfort in different ways."

Kevin glared at her. "Oh, I *understand*."

"It's been four years, Kevin. I have to at least *try* to move on. You have to move on too, Honey, hard as that seems."

Kevin laughed. "Don't you get it? He's a *demolition* expert, Mother. Or maybe you're too drunk to see the irony here."

Jenna opened her mouth to speak, then looked down at her feet where her gaze remained. Kevin realized he'd achieved the desired effect: she was crying. He expected her to say something else, wanted to throw back in her face whatever flaccid platitude about loss and consolation she spewed next. But all that came was a heavy sob and a single, miserable tear falling to his floor as she fled the room.

Kevin got up, locked the door, then put his headphones on and cranked the volume. After an hour or so of brooding, he crept toward the door and listened. Beyond the ringing in his ears, he heard only silence. He went out into the hall and looked over the banister. The downstairs lights were off; only the soft glow of the range-hood bulb was faintly visible from where he stood. He glanced down the hall, just in time to see the light disappear from the crack under his mother's bedroom door. There were sounds coming from that room—sounds that Kevin did not want to hear.

Scowling, he padded downstairs in his socks, made his way down the hall, and stopped at the door all the way at the end on the left. He reached out and grasped the knob, paused, then turned it and crossed the threshold into his father's study.

Kevin wasn't religious, but he thought of this as Frank Heartstone's Chapel. It was a sacred place, untouched by the quotidian, the pedestrian, the *current;* a place of somber enchantment; a place Kevin came to when he was at his most vulnerable to sit amongst the hallowed objects, each connected to his father's venerable memory. It was full of Old, from the furniture to the lamps to the throw rugs, yet for Kevin the place had never assumed the feeling of some stuffy museum. "They were made to be used," his father would say about the things there, adding: "Once, they were loved." On shelves behind latticed doors of the floor-to-ceiling bookcases stood hundreds of volumes: the library that had been the genesis of Kevin's learning. He'd spent countless childhood hours on the rose-colored Empire-style sofa adjacent to the fireplace, studying the forms and details of buildings, the unsmiling faces of daguerreotypes, the Gothic tales of Poe and Lovecraft, the poems of Rilke and Emily Dickinson, the paintings of Dürer and Hieronymus Bosch, while his father sketched fillets and tori. The room was mahogany paneled, with a high ceiling and classical crown molding. Two chairs stood before a fireplace at one end of the room; on the opposite wall was a bay window that overlooked the backyard. Before the window, facing the room, was Frank Heartstone's drafting table, the drawing surface tilted at an angle on cast iron half-moon adjusting wheels. It was the very board on which the great Thomas Farland had designed his domestic and municipal masterpieces.

One of Frank's flannel shirts hung over the creaky wooden swivel chair pushed up against the table. Kevin fingered the shirt's stiffening fabric for a moment before taking a seat. The incomplete blueprint proposal for a new city-commissioned Museum of Science and Industry building his father had been working on was still laid out on the surface, along with a fine-line mechanical pencil, a gum eraser, and the T-square Frank had used since college. A thin veil of dust had settled on the roughly sketched Corinthian columns and window pediments. Kevin could still see his father guiding his pen as if it were a wand along the fine paper, thinking all the while that what he was witnessing was not art, nor work—but magic.

They weren't the only items left in situ. The mug Frank had drunk his last cup of coffee from stood beside these, a black residue thick as resin dried to the bottom. His father's rimless eyeglasses, the left earpiece half folded, lay atop a small filing cabinet to the right of the table. A stack of books was behind them, with titles such as *Fundamental Lines in Nouveau Classicism, Greek and Roman Architectural Rebirth, A Reference Guide to Classical Detail,* along with a host of unmarked leather-bound portfolios containing original lithographs of entablatures, moldings, arches, pilasters, parapets, and porticos.

Once, they were loved, Kevin thought. For years he had relied on relics to connect him with not only his father, but his own notion of the sacred Past. He communed with these objects in his own private inner language, forming a bond that transcended the trivialities of contemporary life, invigorating his passion for erudition while providing him with a sense of quiescence and, paradoxically, place in time. Yet lately these places and things seemed drained of their particular power to console and inspire him, as if the ghosts had vacated them, leaving only brittle, age-worn shells in

40

which he could sense nothing but corrosion and dust. More harrowing still was the notion that they'd never been there in the first place, that he'd created them in order to deal with the truth that, these days, seemed to spread through his mind a little further every day like moss covering a tomb.

He rose, crossed the room, and knelt before the fireplace. Four-year-old issues of the *Lake-Times* and a box of long-stemmed matches lay next to the last box of firewood his father had gathered from the carriage house out back. Kevin balled up a yellowed financial section, stuffed the crumpled pages between the andirons, and then laid three logs across them. Rain began to needle at the bay window as he struck a match and set the paper alight. As the fire grew, so did the storm. Kevin sprawled on the Empire sofa, covering himself with a gray throw draped over the back, and stared at the rising flames. The dry wood crackled in counterpoint to the tick of raindrops on the leaded panes. For the first time in a long time, he felt at ease. At that moment, nothing outside the room mattered. He felt surrounded as if by a carapace, wound in the cocoon of his blanket, and though he wanted to savor the feeling, soon he began to drift off.

*

Jenna sat up in bed, certain that her husband was in the house. He had been in her dream, standing on a ladder in the hall wearing one of his faded red flannel shirts with the sleeves rolled to the forearms. His gelled hair was mussed and powdered with plaster dust. He was tapping on the walls with a hammer as if to find hollow spots, his expression fixed in that engaged, contemplative way that she had found so endearing when they had started dating. In the dream she'd hidden from him, even though she knew in some warped dream-logic that what he was searching for was not in fact a gap between studs, but her. At the same moment she dream-realized this, his hammer punched through the wall, which was mere paper. Frank looked at her suddenly, his eyes dull and flat as nail heads, and then the house began to fall, burying him in a cascade of lath and brick and dust, and then Jenna had awoke, heart thudding, her lungs feeling as if they were filled with dust. Now, as she sat propped against the headboard of the bed they'd shared for a decade, she picked up on scent, one that made the hair on the nape of her neck prickle: wood smoke on the air.

She slid out of bed and put on her robe. Chaz, a shirtless hulk on Frank's former side of the mattress, stirred as she rose, but did not wake. He rolled onto his back and began snoring loudly as Jenna slipped out of the room and followed the scent downstairs. It was definitely smoke, and she knew now where it was coming from. The back-of-the-neck chill crept further along her flesh like tremors. She tread slowly down the hall and stood at the doorway, fingering the silk sleeves of her robe. She hadn't entered this room in over a year. Frank's scent was still strong there; it was almost unbearable how it clung to her clothes after she left. Suddenly she was certain he would be waiting for her. She could see him on the other side of the door, seated at his drafting table, stoic and plaintive as a colonial portrait.

But of course, he wasn't. Instead she found Kevin asleep on that old sofa, its upholstery rash red in the fading firelight. He reminded her of a wounded fawn. She went to him and pulled the blanket up over his shoulders. He was beginning to resemble her less and Frank more the further he moved through adolescence. Perhaps it was part of the reason she felt so wicked and deceitful when he glared at her as he had earlier. But then she did have a man other than Kevin's father in her bed. Being in this room after what she and Chaz had just done filled her with guilt and shame. She knew she wasn't required to feel this way. It was four years since she'd slept with her husband, slept with *anyone* for that matter—a lonesome span of solemn, miserable suffering.

Recently, she'd decided she'd suffered long enough. After a month of being worn down, she'd accepted Chaz's invitation for a drink. Things had happened quickly—more quickly than she'd intended, admittedly—but she didn't regret it. And though the relationship filled one gap in her life, the fissure, already there between her and her son since Frank's death, had widened.

Jenna went to the hearth and watched the flames as they faded to embers. A dust-glazed empty wine bottle stood on the mantel. She picked it up and fingered the cork, remembering the drawing on the bottom. Frank had modified a keystone to include the two lobes of a heart at the top, added the year "2001" in the center, the initial of each of their first names on either side of the symbol, and "HS" underneath it. The air captured within was from their first night in the house; contained both of their mingled breaths, perhaps. The house had been a wreck in those early months before Kevin was born. Initially they had set up small habitable areas throughout, areas that slowly spread to the rest of the interior as Frank meticulously restored the place. He'd done this during his off hours from the architecture firm, where he'd been brought on to fill a Design 1 position, and from dawn to dusk on the weekends. Jenna, a pharmacologist and professed neophyte when it came to Frank's world of astragals, king posts, and raking cornices, helped in the ways she could: painting and sanding and seeding the flower beds. And so they had been partners in bringing the house back to life, in making it theirs.

They'd met during their third term at university. Jenna had fallen in love with Frank's erudite mind and tremendous energy. Frank was slight, like Kevin, but strong and lithe. His hands had been exquisite—slender and purposeful and steady as a surgeon's, adroit with a drawing tool, with the brittle pages of an old book, with her. They married a year after graduation, bought the house on an FHA loan in what was then the undesirable neighborhood of Dovetree. Jenna got a job as research assistant at Chem Corp.—a position that led to her subsequent position with Preventative Solutions. Kevin was born the following autumn, and since that day he and his father had been inseparable. Mother and son loved each other, but the bond Kevin shared with Frank had been almost preternatural, like twins who seem to possess an uncanny proclivity for telepathy. When Frank died, the house had become for Kevin a bizarre proxy for his father. He became obsessed with it, monitored every aspect of its condition, and informed Jenna immediately when something was in need of repair. On many occasions, she'd even let him arrange the details himself with the handyman. So how was she supposed to tell him that she had to sell it?

The expense of keeping up an historic house, paying the bills, and raising a son on a single-parent income had strained her to the brink of financial ruin. The one area her husband had failed them was in not taking out a life insurance policy. With bankruptcy looming, the only way to pay off her debts would be to cash in on this, her only asset—recently appraised at three times what she and Frank had paid for it. Frank had been thrifty, using mostly reclaimed materials for the restoration instead of taking a second mortgage. Nevertheless, the profit she'd make from the sale wouldn't be much—enough to put a security deposit and first month on a rental where they'd live until she was able to save for the down payment on another, smaller house, one most likely in the suburbs. Kevin would understand the economics—he was a smart boy. But he wouldn't accept it, and he would blame her for letting things get this bad. He would see it, along with the appearance of Chaz, as yet another attempt to distance them from Frank. And though it hurt her to admit, Jenna knew that this was in some way true.

For two years after the accident, Kevin had seen a psychologist named Karen Davies, who had diagnosed him with a Cluster A personality disorder characterized by schizoid tendencies. Dr. Davies had also expressed concern with regard to Kevin's pronounced "retrophilia." Frank had of course encouraged a preference for things past in his son.

But when he died, the predilection had turned into a mania for Kevin, who was already maladaptive to the world around him. He had no friends. He didn't talk about girls or what other kids did at school. His grades, surprisingly, had remained exemplary. Lately, though, Kevin had begun to exhibit other aspects from his diagnosed personality disorder, including schizotypal and even paranoid behavior. Without treatment, Jenna feared it would lead to some form of psychosis. She consulted with Dr. Davies and asked her to prescribe an antidepressant for Kevin, preferably Plaiscene— a drug that Jenna not only worked with, but took herself. It was a solution she trusted. Davies had obliged, but it was to no avail: Kevin wouldn't take it.

Jenna looked at him now, asleep in the shadows on the vintage sofa. Other than the way his legs stuck out from under that blanket, which had once covered him so effortlessly, he looked like a child. She wanted to pick him up and carry him to bed as she used to. It felt wrong to leave him in the haunted room with a dying fire. But then he was sleeping so peacefully, so sweetly—she couldn't bear to see those frown lines crease his smooth forehead when he woke and found her standing over him, couldn't face that hard, judgmental glare.

She turned to leave, and as she crossed to the door Jenna thought she felt something behind her: a cold draft accompanied by a slow, raspy sound, like an exhalation of breath. Her skin prickled under her silk robe. *It was only Kevin sighing,* she told herself, drawing the robe tightly around her as she hurried out of the room and closed the door without looking back.

6

Jenna and Chaz were gone when Kevin woke up. His mother had left a note on the island in the kitchen: "Went to brunch, sleepy head. See you in a little while. ♡xxoo"

Kevin crumpled the paper and threw it in the

direction of the trash—he missed, but didn't pick it up. He grabbed a bowl from the cupboard, poured some cereal, and squatted on one of the island stools, gloomily eating as he considered the note. Though he hated to admit it, something about the note had stung him deeply. Was it that they'd gone without him? No; he wouldn't have wanted to even if they'd asked. He decided it was the way she'd offhandedly neglected to mention their argument the night before, glossing over it with cutesiness and little symbols, without apology or regret. Everything about his mother had seemed increasingly fake lately, put-on, detached. It disgusted him, and also made him feel isolated and strangely invisible, like a ghost in his own house. He decided he needed to get out for a while, but the usual places (the library, the local café) didn't excite him. Then a thought occurred to him that made him feel foolish for never thinking before.

Upstairs he dressed quickly, grabbed a handful of change and a few bills from the dwindling can of money he'd earned that summer as a bus boy at one of the neighborhood's overpriced restaurants, looped his bag over his shoulder, and walked out of the house, without leaving a note.

*

The 72 bus picked him on the corner of W. 10th and Carlyle, between two dingy gas stations and a payday loan center occupying an abandoned fast food restaurant. Since it was Saturday, the bus was mostly empty and traffic—both cars and passengers—was light. Kevin pumped a few coins into the meter and slumped into a seat near the back, gazing out the smudged window as the bus grumbled down into the valley. It passed the antediluvian hulk of Holyko Steel whose flare stacks shot jets of flame. According to the papers, the mill would close the following summer if a new investor couldn't be found, bringing to an end one hundred and forty-five years of continuous production. Steel manufacturing was in Kevin's blood; on both his mother's and his father's side were millwrights, stove tenders, cindermen, and grunt laborers who had shoveled coal into sweltering blast furnaces for decades. Their respective families had moved away when the mills started to furlough workers and the neighborhood subsequently began to deteriorate. Frank was raised on the east side of the city and was to date the only of his clan to return to Dovetree. Jenna had grown up in the suburbs like her parents. The latter had been flabbergasted when they learned of their daughter's plans to move back to the old neighborhood.

The bus trundled along the rutted macadam, crossed the scummy Kiksuyapi via drawbridge and continued along Amasa Avenue past a handful of scabby factories, chain restaurants, and churches, merging with Progress Avenue in a section of the city newly christened as "Uptown." It was a notoriously dangerous neighborhood. Neil Memorial Cemetery and its nearby older neighbor Treestone occupied a combined eight blocks there in what was once a rural area far outside the city limits. In the intervening century, blocks of working-class houses and micro-industrial sites had filled the gap between downtown and farm country. Like everything else in Still City, they'd risen quickly, and then steadily declined, so that by the turn of the new millennium the majority of Uptown's houses and small manufacturing buildings had been abandoned for twenty years or more. Many were razed, and in their place low-income housing went up on the large city-owned tracts—purposely isolated, or so it seemed, from the few remaining affluent sections of town. Kevin thought of his mother, sipping mimosas with Chaz at Blue Pier Point. Wouldn't she freak out if she saw him stepping off the 72 onto the garbage-strewn sidewalk before Neil Memorial's main gate! The thought made one corner of his mouth twitch up as he started down the crushed gravel road between the first few rows of graves.

47

As if in accordance with the calendar, the weather had shifted from auburn late-autumn warmth to a steely December chill. Kevin walked along a curving path toward Section 98 located at the extreme southeastern corner of the grounds. The cemetery was mostly modern, with the oldest graves dating from the 1930s. The monuments were primarily laser-cut granite or lawn-level metal plaques with bronze vases full of plastic flowers. Kevin's father's stone was one of the only above-ground markers in its group: a pink granite slab with HEARTSTONE engraved at the top, and below it FRANK L. and JENNETTE C. Kevin remembered how angry he'd been when as a child he saw that his own name was absent from the monument. When he'd asked why, his mother frowned darkly and said: "You're too young, Kevin."

"Too young too die?" he'd responded.

"That, and what if you get married one day?"

"What's that got to do with anything?"

"You might want to be buried next to your wife."

"I want to be next to my father!" he'd shouted, and ran up to his room in a teary rage.

Now, as he brushed the twigs and dead leaves away from the base of the stone, he pondered whether that moment had been the genesis of the rancorous feelings he felt toward his mother. He stared down at her name, her year open-ended. Not his father's, though: those numbers were final, inexorable—quite literally, set in stone. The headstone had settled slightly to the right, and a chunk was gone from the upper left corner, knocked off perhaps by a piece of ejecta thrown by a riding lawnmower. Kevin located the piece, regarded it, then put it in his pocket. Grass had grown in lushly again over the area where the earth had been turned over to make room for his father's casket, but the outline of the grave where the filled ground had settled was still faintly visible. He plucked a candy wrapper snagged in the browned evergreen wreath his mother had placed last Christmas and stuck it in his bag. He and his mother came here rarely—on major holidays or Frank's birthday, Jenna sometimes on their

48

wedding anniversary. He usually felt some swell of emotion when he stood here—sadness, anger, love. Today he felt only the cold biting his face, finding its way through his thin jacket. He did not cry, though he tasted tears in the back of his throat. It frightened him somewhat, this no-reaction.

They're gone . . . they don't linger, and they don't come back.

It was a thought that followed him out of Neil Memorial Cemetery. He'd planned on spending most of the day sitting at his father's grave, but that empty feeling, the one that told Kevin his father wasn't there even though Frank Heartstone's body was, threatened to overwhelm him in a way he couldn't presently deal with. He wanted to leave, but the 72 wouldn't be back for another forty-five minutes, and this wasn't an ideal part of town to be wandering around alone. Then he thought about Treestone.

He'd always wanted to go there, had gazed fascinatedly at the overgrown wreck of it through the car window on the few occasions he and his mother had driven past. The cemetery, according to a plaque attached to one of the stone columns of the main entrance arch, was a registered historical landmark. Nevertheless it was a shambles, from its stained Gothic gate to its rambling acres of weedy, neglected plots littered with trash and toppled headstones. Rust speckled the wrought iron perimeter fence like a coating of spring pollen. Still City's founders, mayors, business tycoons, and artists were buried here. Despite the cemetery's illustrious pedigree, the majority of the mausoleums were either boarded up or, more disquietingly, had their entrances sealed with concrete blocks and cement. The doors of many others stood wide open, half ripped off their antiquated hinges and tagged with graffiti.

Things here were wild, mangled, shattered, in the aftermath of violence. True decay. There were dangers— vagrants, squatters, vandals, drug addicts—but Kevin wasn't thinking of them now. Nor was he scared, in the traditional sense, of the place as some spooky B-movie horror setting where the dead returned to eat the brains of the living or haunt them in the form of half-decayed phantoms. To most, a weathered old graveyard was all about ghosts, the names pickpocketed from the hand-incised fieldstones and whispered over Ouija boards on Halloween night. Kevin knew that none of the people interred therein would have wanted to be remembered as monsters or specters. They had walked under the same sun, breathed the same air, turned over the same dirt to plant seeds and lay foundations. And how heavy that dirt was now, piled upon them, as it was on Frank Heartstone. It was a weight Kevin couldn't consider without feeling overwhelmed by a sense of claustrophobic panic as he trekked along the tangled paths, watched by a crow or two and a few weather-worn angels, pinions snapped off, faces stained. There was evidence of squatters everywhere. A wet yellow tent lay half collapsed like a torn sail before a blackened fire scar in the dirt. The makeshift pit was ringed with the stones of chrisom children. Rows of beer cans and drug paraphernalia stood atop a nearby chest tomb. It was plain why the transients hadn't stayed long: it stunk here. No ghostly green haze drifted through Treestone, but Kevin didn't need it to recognize the astringent tang of melting plastic.

There was a massive fountain at the center of the cemetery that, like the rest of the place, was overgrown and crumbling. The pool basin was filled with litter and dead vegetation and large chunks of broken monuments along with six or so inches of stagnant water. A young but well-established pin oak had sprung up from the middle of the fount. Brown crackled leaves, still clinging to its dormant limbs, rattled in the rising wind, the sound eerily reminiscent of what the water must have once sounded like as it spurted out of the cracked surmounting urn. A path lined with fractured white pavers ringed the fountain. Several stone benches stood at intervals along this perimeter. Kevin sat on one of these, crossed his arms over the thin jacket, and shivered. It wasn't only the cold making him uncomfortable, but the mounting certainty that he was being watched. There were sounds here, noises other than the leaves and crows and the intermittent scuttling of rodents in the tall grass.

All at once it occurred to him where he was: in a disintegrating cemetery in the heart of Uptown, without a phone and without anyone knowing he was here. If something happened to him, no one would look here. He took out his pocket watch, flipped up the palm-worn lid, and checked the time: still nearly half an hour until the bus returned. The wind was picking up; he heard a distant groan of thunder. The sky was turning a soupy gray, like the lake in winter, but it wasn't clear whether the storm would be rain or snow. When it came a few minutes later it was a mix of the two, cold and sharp and biting. Drawing his hood up, Kevin ran to the nearest mausoleum for shelter. The tomb was large, the entrance flanked by a pair of inverted torches. The name above it, engraved in low relief, read CARDINAL. One green oxidized door was thrown back against the façade, the other remained closed.

Kevin approached it slowly despite the rain, regarding the black opening with trepidation. Anyone might be in there—a possibility only marginally more frightening than what certainly *was* within. He hovered in the doorway, listening, waiting for his senses to discern something in the dark. There wasn't any smell or contemporary refuse, no bongs made from empty two-liter soda bottles, no crushed Old Steed tallboy beer cans, no blankets crusted with blood, food, shit. No sign that anyone other than the person for whom the sepulcher had been made for resided within. Even so, he refused to turn his back to that blind space. He set his bag down on the threshold and stood, spine pressed to jamb, watching the storm, occasionally glancing into the darkness behind him. Gradually the sleet lessened, leaving just the rain pattering softly and steadily on the roof of the tomb, invoking a trance-like state in Kevin, who forgot about the void on his left until he felt a hand reach out of it and settle on his shoulder.

He leapt out of the doorway, tripped over the strap of

51

his bag, and fell on his face in the slush-covered grass. A second later he was up and scuttling away from the entrance. He looked back as he ran, seeing at first only blackness. Then, slowly, a figure emerged. It was a girl around his age, or so he thought. She wore a flounced black taffeta dress with short sleeves, black lace mitts, and a necklace of pale orange beads. A pair of black silk ribbons tied into large loose bows bound her long dark hair on either side of her face. Her skin was a waxy gray/yellow, her expression solemn and dolorous, her eyes so green they seemed to radiate the color.

Kevin fled in a random direction, deep into Treestone. He paused near a shagbark hickory, heaving breaths. The rain had let up, but his clothes, especially his jeans and his shoes, were drenched. He reached for his bag, remembered where he'd left it, and let out a moan. In it wasn't only his commonplace book, but the rest of his money. He scanned for the closest exit and spotted the rear entrance—thirty yards or so northeast of where he stood. This section of the cemetery was flatter and older. The white oaks and chestnuts and weeping hemlocks were well-established and the stones were wordless headboards. As he crossed the grounds, heading in the direction of the main road, Kevin noticed there were holes in the graves—great, gaping mouths tunneled up through the dirt. At first he'd thought they had been dug by animals, but as he stared down into one of the clotted throats, he realized it had been bored by something trying to get *out*, not in. He flashed on the man he'd chased across the footbridge. Then he thought of the girl; he could still feel her touch on his shoulder. That hand had been cold and hard.

Something stirred behind him. For a moment, Kevin thought it was only the rain recommencing. Then he heard susurrations, voices. He started walking again, deliberately slowly, then faster and faster until he was leaping over the black gaps in the ground, half expecting a pair of pale, rotted hands to reach up and snag him by the ankles. By the time he reached the road he was sprinting. Reaching the exit, he found it shut and chained, though there was enough play between the gates for Kevin to squeeze through. He looked over his shoulder as he fled. There was movement at the gate, a host of figures gathered where he'd been only seconds before. He ran two blocks, then cut down East 74th, which would lead him back to Progress Avenue and the main entrances of Treestone and Neil Memorial.

It was a typical east side street, lined with ramshackle row houses interspersed with empty lots, like a jaw with teeth missing. On one of these vacant tracts some kids were using a twisted curtain rod and a broken broom handle to smash the windshield of a rusted sedan. Kevin walked quickly, keeping his eyes on the fractured pavement. There were whispers coming from the porches and incomprehensible shouts that may or may not have been directed at him. *Walk fast and don't look up,* he thought. Halfway down, a man approached him on the sidewalk. Kevin moved into the street to avoid him, but the man followed. He stank of cheap gin and body odor rank as a restaurant grease trap and was mumbling something about a lost lottery ticket. Kevin said he didn't have it, but the man gripped him by the jacket, his calcified nails raking the thin material, and began screaming profanities three inches from Kevin's face. A moment later a car, glass tinted black, booming bass rattling the trunk, turned onto 74th headed in their direction. The windows rolled down as it coasted toward them. For a second, Kevin was certain he was about to be jumped—would have in any other case, he thought later, had he not appeared to be consorting with a crackhead. When the car passed, Kevin threw an elbow into the drunk's ribs. The man let out a gasp like a deflating tire but didn't let go, so Kevin threw another jab, this one twice as hard, and the man skidded backwards with a wail into an overflowing trash bin, making an obscene clatter. The kids by the car stopped smashing and started shouting. They came at Kevin with their makeshift weapons held high. Other voices rose: the street was alive, roused by the powerful aphrodisiac of violence. The car with the darkened windows revved its engine, tires squealing as it turned around.

Kevin ran, teeth clenched, eyes bulging, feet squelching in his soggy shoes. His mother's voice came to him again like some latent prophecy, and he wondered blackly if, when they found him, she would end up adding his name to the Heartstone family monument after all.

He made it to the end of the street and rounded the corner at the same moment a police car was driving past. Instinctively, Kevin stopped running, though the throng behind him didn't. The cruiser cut a diagonal path between them; its lights went on, its siren emitted a series of blips.

*

Kevin walked the ninety blocks home through the roughest section of Still City, huddling in doorways to wait out the intermittent rain and hiding behind dumpsters or in abandoned buildings when he sensed trouble. Progress Avenue, from roughly East 130th to East 30th, was a no-man's-land forsaken generations ago by both private investors and the local government. The so-called gentrification and urban renewal reinvigorating downtown had not extended, and most likely never would extend, this far. Even when state money was allotted, it was invariably used to tear down "blighted structures" rather than reinvest in a community of nearly 50,000. It took Kevin three hours to navigate the wilderness of commercial and residential ruin. He'd seen photos of what this stretch had looked like in the nineteenth century when it had been one of the most affluent and beautiful thoroughfares in the world. Its current broken state—the patched infrastructure and rows of architectural palimpsests—mirrored his own feelings of hopelessness and futility. As he scurried from street to street, shivering, teeth chattering, that oddly detached feeling of not belonging to his time, of somehow *living dead,* solidified in him, hard and defiant as these archaic buildings that, despite years of neglect, refused to succumb. Near East 36th, Kevin passed a house with flaking paint and a collapsing spindle-work porch, its roof sagging like a frown. Its expression reminded him of the girl from Treestone. He saw her face receding into the tomb—into that space meant to hold her in eternal black. It made him think: what was going on here? Was some cult parading around the city dressed like dead Victorians? Or was this really something . . . else? He pondered this as he made his way along the old river road, a single-lane passage that followed the loop of the Kiksuyapi, bending slightly to the east before continuing west again. Kevin crossed another of the turn-of-the-century drawbridges linking the two sections of the city, stepped onto the river's west bank, then continued up West 3rd Street, which led at last back to Dovetree.

It was dusk by the time he reached Garfield Park. The nightly stink of the PS plant had already crept into the neighborhood, the low green fog accompanied by a steady drizzle. He had been hoping his mother and Chaz would still be out, but Jenna's car was in the driveway. Chaz's, at least, was gone. Kevin opened and closed the front door quietly, hoping he might be able to sneak up to his room. At the sound of the clicking latch his mother rushed into the foyer. She looked frantic, her hair down and wild, her eyes red-lined and puffy.

"Where have you been? We drove around for *hours* looking for you. Why didn't you leave a note?"

Kevin had had a lie ready about being at the library and missing the bus. But all of a sudden he wanted to tell the truth. He *wanted* her to know where he'd gone—on his own.

"I went to see Dad."

His mother regarded him steadily for a long, silent moment. "Kevin, your father is not there."

"What do you mean, *not there?* Of course he is."

"Kevin, that's just a body."

Kevin looked at her, incredulous. She hadn't even said *his* body—no, just *a* body. The words had cut him, and now he wanted to cut her back.

"I wish it had been you."

He watched her face, waiting for the words to detonate like a missile on its target, but Jenna's expression didn't change. "I know you do."

Kevin looked at her, stunned. He realized that what he had said had rebounded, and it made him cold all over. He wanted to take it back, but he couldn't. There was nothing left to say.

He went to his room and sat numbly at his desk. He took the hunk of granite from his father's headstone out of his pocket, pressed it to his lips, then set it atop the desk beside his pencil cup. He wished he had his commonplace book. He wondered who would find it, if they would read all his private thoughts, and whether they would mock him and laugh at him. He stared at the spines of his books, but for once Kevin didn't feel like thinking about learning, or the past, or death.

Exhausted, he lay on his bed, hoping for transient oblivion, but instead dreamt of corpses marching through the city toward Central Square. His father was among them, dressed in that awkward funeral suit, his flesh newspaper gray, his eyes blank as a Roman bust. Kevin called to him from some high and omniscient vantage-point, and Frank Heartstone seemed to hear him, glancing up in Kevin's direction as he moved past along with the procession of the dead. Kevin cried his father's name again and again, his voice a shrill scream echoing down the long avenue of ruined skyscrapers. In his bedroom, the scream was small and pathetic; a mere whimper in the dark.

7

A fortnight later, under the shrouded eye of a new moon, a figure moved through the falling snow across the Heartstone lawn. It approached the front stoop slowly, cautiously, laid something in front of the door, and then skittered off again.

II.

"Any relic of the dead is precious, if they were valued living."

EMILY BRONTË
Wuthering Heights

1

They ventured out one by one, each in their own time, each when they were ready. They wanted to know what had become of their homes, their businesses, *their* city. They wandered through the vast and incomprehensible sprawl, guided by the few remaining landmarks recognizable to them. For most, the places they sought were altered or hideously decayed or altogether vanished. They wondered if their family members had returned as well, and went looking for them in neighboring cemeteries, only to find the grounds undisturbed and the doors of the crumbling mausoleums sealed. How they mourned then, standing at the flowerless, dilapidated memorials of their loved ones, long since dust.

Julia Reese, a spinster who had died in her eighty-sixth year three days before the turn of the twentieth century, went to the waterfront park in which she and her beloved James had walked during their courtship. James died in the cholera epidemic the summer before they were to be married, and Julia had spent sixty years wandering those paths they had strolled together, pondering what might have been. Now, instead of the familiar rows of handsome oaks and flowerbeds bright as barrelfuls of spilled jewels, Julia found a used car lot and a defunct chicken restaurant on the hallowed spot where James had proposed marriage.

Captain Sebastian Kline of the *W. M. DeStill*—the flagship of the Northcoast Fishery's mercantile fleet—stood at the end of the city pier, collar raised though he couldn't feel the cold, his bare bone jaw set as he regarded the foamy water lapping the rotted dock pilings jutting up from the surface of the lake. He was trying to recall the oily stench of perch and walleye guts. Though he'd detested it in life (the way it clung to his skin like wet cloth) he wished more than anything now that he could be allowed one waft so that it might aid his dulled memory in rebuilding what had long since been razed: the processing sheds, the seine nets, the boats in dry dock in winter. But there were only the gulls, always the gulls, and the churning water, the same brown as the grave mud clinging to his burial rags.

Charles Mills, a teller at the Carver Street Bank, had been a fastidious man in life who had valued punctuality above all other virtues. When he Woke, the first thing he'd felt for in the blackness was his pocket watch—stopped at the moment of his death and duly interred with him as directed in his will on the vest chain of his funeral suit. He'd risen promptly, though a little stiffly, walked out of his tomb as if it were the front door of his former house, brushing the dust off and pulling web from his hair as he strode down the street in the early morning sun on his way to work. But when he arrived at 76 Carver Street, he found not the little Federal-style brick building in which he'd spent thirty-three years managing accounts, but a towering edifice made of steel and shadowy glass. In one of those murky reflective panels, Charles gaped at the shriveled face looking back at him. Fastidious not longer, he walked back to his tomb, barred the doors from within, and never came out again.

Yet some—a very rare few indeed—found their former residences not only intact, but just as they'd left them. Margaret Worthington was one of these. She'd crept through the hardened landscape of concrete and wires and hordes of blinding lights and shrieking machines, keeping in the shadows and diving onto the ground in a brusque and decidedly unlady-like manner when she heard approaching voices. For days she journeyed like this, navigating the urban alien plain until at last she arrived at the village of Greenlawn. It had been established in the mid-nineteenth century as a fresh air Eden, far from the foulness of the city. Now, exhaust fumes from the highway mingled with the smell of pine and the faint piscine stink of the lake. But for the most part Greenlawn remained as it had been in Margaret's time. The trees were towering now, and much of the vacant land was occupied by huge and oddly geometric houses, but the paved roads led in the same directions as they had in the days when horses and carriages passed down them. And when at last she saw with her blazing green eyes the lit windows and smoke trailing from the chimneys of the Italianate country house built by her husband John one hundred and fifty-seven years ago, she felt something she hadn't since Waking, or for that matter, hadn't realized she was capable of in this renewed existence: a swell of love. It had begun to snow an hour or so earlier, big pillowy flakes, and for a long time she merely stood and watched them fall around the grand old place. How unchanged it was! The current occupants had even draped it in wintery garland and bows, just as she used to. Margaret walked the path leading to the front stairs and stepped onto the veranda. A rocking chair stood at the far left end, similar to the one in which she rocked each of her four boys when they were infants. She'd lived to see all of them buried. Now Margaret went to the chair, sat, and began rocking slowly, humming "Slumber, My Darling."

And then there was Thomas Farland, the leading architect of the second half of the nineteenth century, the man responsible for establishing Still City as one of the nation's premier modern metropoles. His duties had extended beyond merely designing buildings: he was also a civil engineer and had held the title of associate city planner, working closely with that department on a number of municipal upgrades that transformed the little commercial fishing port into an industrial powerhouse. Thomas had been one of the first to venture out after Waking, thrilled for the opportunity to see how his "darlings," as he called his structures, had fared through the ages. After all, he'd built them well—for his customers as well as for posterity.

He started out in the direction of Progress Avenue— the street that had made his name synonymous with prestige and affluence. In the burgeoning city, young architects had vied ruthlessly for commissions. Thomas had himself designed forty of the three hundred grand houses on Still City's millionaires' mile, whose occupants made up a third of wealthiest individuals in the world. They had come to him with dreams of urban palaces, surrounded by vast contemplative spaces boasting idyllic grounds that featured erumpent fountains, classical statuary, and sunken gardens— all hedged in by elaborate wrought iron fences. Each was different from the next: storybook chateaus stood beside Second Empire monstrosities that neighbored Italianate and Romanesque fantasies. There was even an Octagonal house. And yet, despite the close proximity of the mansions not only to one another but the city itself, a pastoral tranquility reigned along the Progress Avenue. When streetcars began to appear downtown, the lines were diverted so that they did not pass down the avenue. For decades, only the clatter of carriage wheels and the clomp of horses' hooves echoed off the towering ashlar walls, a temporary disturbance in the grandiose stillness, like the buzz of a single passing insect.

Thomas recalled the old scene as he walked under the moonlight: the way the sun passed through the leafy tops of the rows of great elms and the soft gas flames in the street lanterns at night; the men and women on pleasure strolls, resplendently dressed; the coaches and the paved paths leading from the avenue to the porte-cochères. Now, he pictured every one of his darlings, recalling each imposing and magnificent countenance set upon acres of meticulous lawns. What great men dwelt in them now, he wondered? How refined and enlightened they must be! How he longed to meet them—to sit in the sumptuous rooms of his own design, sipping brandy and learning of all the miraculous advancements and discoveries of the last century. He felt some shame in entertaining this vanity, for certainly he was seeking at least a modicum of praise. Then he thought: scruples be damned! This was no occasion for modesty. If they invited him in, he would gladly partake of their company and revel in their accolades. Why shouldn't they celebrate him?

Yet the closer he got to the edge of the district the more anxious he became. It was shocking, bewildering even, how far the city had expanded since his time—from downtown all the way to East 70th Street where Treestone

Cemetery, established on a formerly remote and rural setting, stood. When he looked at the metal-clad houses and the massive brick shells of deserted factories through which a disconcerting green mist floated, doubts began to creep in with regard to the supposed "refinement" of this age. Decay and dissonance, not perspicacious amelioration, seemed the most prevalent aspects of this modern society. He began to muse darkly about the state of his creations as he waded through the alien refuse scattered indiscriminately everywhere. Would they be altered? Surely repairs would have been necessary over time. Perhaps some of them had undergone the inevitable small renovation or two. But he would recognize them—he was sure of it. Not even the fiercest natural disaster, after all, could pull down a Thomas Farland.

He was only a few blocks away now. He began to trot, his heart a still and shriveled thing, but his revived mind reeling with excitement and anticipation. He passed under a rusted railroad bridge covered in multi-colored illegible scrawl. On the other side would be East 40th and the Wren House— the last design he'd finished before he died. He hadn't lived to see it completed, and it seemed fitting that it would be the first he would behold now upon his Return. But as he emerged, he didn't see the classical columns and the ornate entablature of the Greek Revival Wren, only a sprawling, weedy lot of cracked asphalt surrounded by a sagging chain-link perimeter fence. For a moment Thomas's glowing eyes fixed on the spot, then swept slowly down the long, concrete corridor, filled not with rows of grand manors but block after block of squat, ascetic buildings, each as dull and monochromatic as the next. They huddled at the edges of the sidewalks, their façades cragged and filthy as the faces of beggars. Lofty, desiccated wooded posts strung with drooping wire had taken the place of the hearty elms on either side of the avenue. On every other one of these hung a rusted, arcing arm casting dirty yellowy light through cataract-like lenses.

Thomas staggered forward like a man walking

through a war zone. They were gone—all of them. Maass Mansion; the Wren, Skrdla, and Binford houses. Even Carter Court—a Tudor revival that had occupied a prominent lot boasting a higher elevation than the rest—had been razed. On that now hirsute hill was a billboard with an image of a woman with a dazed look that read *"Plaiscene* means *peace of mind."*

Thomas wandered toward downtown, scanning for even the smallest vestige of his time. With each street sign he would pause, superimposing the images from his mind over the current scene until his mental faculty surrendered to sorrow and indignation. This was a pernicious age, he decided: mechanical, artless, hedonistic even. At East 20th, a wide median began down the center of the avenue. Thomas kept in the shadows, glaring at the slovenly, unkempt hordes waiting to board one those dreadful steel-sided omnibuses. Not a single respectable one among them. There had been poverty, debauchery, scandalous depravity in his century just like any other. But this lot, despite their manifold conveniences and the rapid accessibility of both transportation and information, appeared more base and ignorant than even the most indolent Victorian.

Despite his dismay he pressed on, eager to learn whether or not his contributions at the heart of town had survived. He kept to the alleys and other dark passages, which eventually led him to Central Square. The buildings there were colossi—immense, dumfounding to behold. Thomas hid behind a dumpster, gaping incomprehensibly up at them. He did not notice his Central Commerce building right away. At ninety-six meters, it had been the tallest building in the nation at the time of its completion in 1881. Now, flanked by a pair of glass towers four times its size, the clay-colored masonry was stained black and a huge "For Lease" sign hung over the three central lancet windows of the twentieth and highest floor. Thomas remembered how modern it had once looked, looming over its brick- and timber-framed contemporaries. How archaic it appeared now with its arches, white granite belt courses, and decorative cornice. Adornment was not a priority for the architects of the prevailing high-rise edifices. Size—not stateliness—seemed the objective of the contemporary draftsmen.

Nevertheless, Thomas gazed upon his once unparalleled accomplishment with boundless pride. It had remained, *survived*. He wanted more than anything to pass under the ornate architrave of the main entrance; to mount the marble central stair; to wander through the expansive mahogany-paneled offices, and, finally, stand on the observation deck, which in its day had offered an unparalleled view of the lake and islands as well as the city itself. Perhaps seeing it all from such a height would offer some perspective, a unifying means with which he might understand these people.

But this was impossible. The square was already thrumming with cars and dour-faced early-morning commuters, and Thomas, in his state, did not dare attempt to get any closer. Instead he continued west as he had before, keeping to the shadowy paths but this time moving away from the city. For there, on Belkin Street in Still City's once illustrious West End, stood the jewel of his career and his most beloved darling: his own home.

In his will, Thomas had left the house and the three acres of rolling grounds on which it stood to the city with a requirement that it be utilized as the official mayor's residence. The purpose of this had been to keep it out of the hands of property speculators and commercial investors who sought expansion beyond the then shallowly established city limits. For the many great houses on the city's doorstep this of course would mean a wholesale razing. Thomas had foreseen this and shrewdly included a stipulation stating that by accepting his estate and agreeing to his terms, the city would be legally bound to the condition in his will, and thus have no authority to tear down the house at any time, whether or not the mayor chose to live there. This was consummated when Still City formally absorbed the estate as government property after Thomas's death. And indeed, seventeen of the city's subsequent mayors had in fact lived there, the honor of inhabiting the former residence of the great architect one of the central privileges that came along with the office.

And during the declining years, the surrounding houses had indeed succumbed to the wrecking ball. Storefronts and small-scale manufacturing buildings went up in their place, were themselves torn down, and replaced by low-income housing projects, convenience store gas stations, and fast-food restaurants. When Glenn Grover was elected in 1967, he became the first mayor in seventy-five years not to eschew the mayoral mansion, opting to remain at his current home, nestled safely in the suburbs, for the duration of his term. Thomas's house, located at the heart of the forlorn West End, became an object of derision for the neighboring slums—a scapegoat for the crippling poverty and lack of employment opportunity. The mansion rapidly declined, hosting an array of unspeakable acts of debauchery and vandalism so that by the time Thomas came upon it, now fifty years abandoned, it was little more than a masonry shell, its central tower collapsed, its brackets and window caps hacked away, its low, ivy-patterned iron fence rusted and spattered with graffiti. A bright orange CONDEMNED sign was pasted to the front entrance, and another, nailed to a post driven into the tire- and trash-strewn front lawn, read "R. F. Demolition." In the end the city had found a way to circumvent his will: by declaring his once grand darling a nuisance—a hazard to the community. They would pull it down, stone by stone; the setting of all his happy years with Charlotte and the children. It would vanish like the others.

He'd created this place for them, a domestic sanctuary where anguish and grief—two hallmarks of his age—would hold no dominion. As he looked upon the lawn, Thomas could still see Effie and Nellie at tea with their dolls (Effie with her father's dark hair and olive eyes, Nellie fair and fragile like her mother). He looked at the shattered windows of his bedchamber and thought of his dear Charlotte, of the

66

intimacy and tenderness they'd shared there.

But the stained façade and trashed grounds offered no lasting succor. His wife had been cremated, and his daughters, married and living in neighboring counties, had long since disintegrated beside their husbands. Of those gilded days only Thomas and his house remained, brothers in decay, and he found that all he could do was something his age had had a particular proclivity for.

Mourn.

2

From Channel 9 "News at 9" segment.

(*Tim Spears, Lead Anchor*): "Eerie goings-on at one of the city's oldest graveyards. Yesterday News Channel 9 received a tip from a nearby resident who reported several disturbed plots in Still City's historic Treestone Cemetery. Here's our own Roberta Denton with more on this chilling developing story."

(*Several video shots of empty graves and open tombs with the following dialogue overdubbed.*)

(*Roberta Denton, Reporter*): "Headstone toppling, tomb looting, even . . . body snatching? They are macabre, almost unthinkable crimes, but that's exactly what's been going on in one of the east side's most historic burying grounds. Myron Willis, a resident of nearby Sunny Start Apartments, was cutting through the cemetery on his way to a convenient store when he noticed countless holes in the ground before tombstones and doors swung wide on mausoleums."

(*Myron Willis, 58, retired security guard*): "I thought they finally doin' somethin' 'bout this place. Maintenance and whatnot. Then I realized there's somethin' *else* goin' on here."

(*Roberta Denton*): "'Something else' indeed, as further investigation of the desecrated sights revealed *missing remains* . . . many of which had been interred well over a century ago and include prominent figures from Stilly City's Industrial Era. Cemetery officials are shocked and perplexed by what they are calling a 'well-coordinated act of vandalism.'"

(*Eric Lester, Treestone Cemetery Preservation Society President*): "We have no idea who is responsible or what their motivations are, but we suspect that it was not an act committed by a single individual."

(*Roberta Denton*): "When asked how such a mass desecration could have taken place under cemetery officials' noses, Mr. Lester had this to say."

(*Eric Lester*): "We are not on-site day to day." (*Cut in—omniscient voice of Ms. Denton from off camera*) "What about guards? Who patrols the grounds and opens and closes the gates?" (*Eric Lester, continued*) "Look, funds have been cut, okay? The new federal administration has decreased historical preservation budgets by ninety percent. The money simply isn't there, even to pay for essentials."

(*Roberta Denton*): "But local residents like Tamikia Barnes say the condition of the cemetery has been a longstanding issue, going back *years* rather than months, and that Treestone as a result has become a dangerous haven for crime and other suspicious activity."

(*Tamikia Barnes, 24, fast-food cook*): "Been like that ever since I lived here. Twenty-two years. Nothin' but crackheads, homeless, prostitutes—it's a scary place. I don't let my kids go near it."

(*Roberta Denton*): "It's not just the threat of crime that's alarming. A study of police reports filed over the last four years shows nearly a hundred complaints concerning suspicious trucks dumping assorted refuse and *liquid waste* in the cemetery, nearby vacant lots, and even in the yards of occupied houses in the surrounding area."

(*Tamikia Barnes*): "You know what? It's the same thing all the time around here. They wanna blame someone *else* rather then clean it up themselves. The city don't care 'bout us. They don't give a s***. Ain't nobody respects this neighborhood. But we part of this city too, you know? This ain't no toilet."

(*Roberta Denton—standing before Treestone's gates at dusk*):

68

"But apparently word *has* reached city officials, as just within the last few hours the main entrances of the cemetery have been chained and padlocked. In addition, a notice by the Still City Police Department has been posted, as you can see here, warning against trespassing. (*Camera zooms in on several signs stapled to a plywood barrier; the camera follows Roberta Denton's hand as she discusses each one.*) More interesting still are these 'Restricted Access' and 'Surveillance Area' signs, suggesting the involvement of more than one state department, perhaps even federal agencies.

"So what is really going on here? News Channel 9 has contacted the mayor's office regarding the closure, but we've yet to obtain any definitive explanation for what has taken place during the last forty-eight hours. At any rate, you can bet that we will be following events closely and report further developments as breaking news. There's more to this story than we're being told. Back to you, Tim."

(*Tim Spears*): "Thank you, Roberta. This report coincides with a recent spate of purported 'corpse' sightings around several area neighborhoods. Still City Police have received a whopping *five hundred* complaints, along with some disturbing video footage, concerning these so-called walking dead. Many believe this is a ramping up of an elaborate hoax that began around Halloween and has escalated over the last several weeks. Just who they are, and what they hope to accomplish, remains to be seen." (*Jazz music cue signaling commercial break*) "Up next, is your dog trying to tell you something about your cholesterol? We'll talk to a leading expert who claims your canine's intuition may help lower your risk of heart disease . . ."

3

Dovetree had been strangely quiet since the story broke. Business at the local bars and restaurants was slow. Animals were kept indoors. People stayed home unless it was necessary to venture out, waiting for whatever was going on to resolve. As Kevin watched incredulously the home-shot clips on the news of figures dressed in rotted grave cerements, he wondered if he was the only one who suspected that this wasn't merely some copycat trend. *Still City—the town where the Dead walk.* Not a slogan the tourism board would be adopting in the near future.

Kevin and his mother had hardly spoken during last two weeks, mostly because of the confessions made in the foyer, but also because she'd begun working twelve-hour shifts and half-days on weekends. Something, apparently, was going on at Preventative Solutions—a notion that only reinforced Kevin's suspicions of the tie between the green miasma and the throng he'd seen gathered at the Treestone gate.

Christmas loomed—only a few days away—but no one bothered to decorate or get a tree.

On the Saturday before holiday break, Kevin woke early with the lingering impressions of a bad dream. He lay in bed awhile, gazing up at ice-crystal shadows embroidering a scalene triangle of brilliant sunlight on the ceiling of his room. They reminded him of the lace of the dress on the girl from the tomb. A thought occurred to him that made him sit up, slide out of bed (hair sticking up, one pant leg rolled to his knee from kicking at the covers in his sleep), and go to one of his bookshelves. The reference volumes were second shelf from the bottom. He drew one of these out—*A Survey of Victorian Fashions*—sat on the side of his desk chair, and began paging through it with those few details he'd glimpsed fixed in his mind.

About a quarter of the way in, Kevin stopped on an image of a young girl in a black silk dress with flounced skirts and braiding on the sleeves. The subject wore a string of round, uniform beads, similar to one Kevin had seen around the neck of the girl from the tomb. Those had been pale orange. He flipped to the jewelry section of the book, perusing the necklaces until he found one that was that same salmon shade. The caption said it was coral.

Kevin set the book down, went back to the reference shelf, and got his symbolism dictionary. Under the "gemstones" section he read that the ancient Romans used coral as a protective amulet to guard against disease in children. The talisman had failed to protect the girl he'd seen, but she'd been laid to rest with it anyway. Perhaps it had been one of her favorite belongings. Who was she? He recalled the word engraved above the mausoleum door. From his studies, he knew the name "Cardinal" to be synonymous with magistrates and railroads, particularly in the mid-1850s when the latter became ubiquitous in the city. This also fit with the projected timeframe during which the girl had lived and died. Kevin wanted to go back to Treestone, to that eroding primary source. He needed to see the tomb again—not that he planned on seeing *her*, but then, what if?

He put some jeans on, pulled his father's hooded sweatshirt over the T-shirt he'd slept in, and grabbed a pair of beat-up sneakers. His mother usually slept late on the weekends, so it was a surprise when he stepped out into the hall and heard the shower running. He didn't know why she was up so early but supposed it had something to do with Chaz—another brunch, maybe some Christmas shopping. He didn't really care. It gave him the chance to slip out unseen.

Downstairs as he was getting his coat from the foyer closet, something in the dining room caught his eye. His bag was lying on the gate leg table. For a long time Kevin stared at it as if it were a ghost. Crossing the room slowly, he lifted it by the strap and examined it. The material was streaked with mud, but all his things were inside: his commonplace book, the library books, even the snacks he'd brought with him the day he'd abandoned it.

Upstairs, he heard the shower turn off and, almost at the same moment, a car pulling into the driveway. Kevin peeked out the window. Chaz's diesel pickup was parking behind Jenna's sedan. Kevin grabbed the bag and started for the back door.

*

He walked to the opposite end of the neighborhood and caught the 93. The bus followed the highway, continued through downtown, and stopped at the main hub where Kevin would pick up the 72. It was delayed forty minutes due to an accident on the inner belt, so he waited on one of the steel benches in the lobby. He took out his commonplace book, still in disbelief that he had it back. As he opened it, something fell out into his lap: a yellowy parchment with his name penned across the front in formal, old-fashioned script. His hands shook as he held it up. It seemed, paradoxically, old and new—an erstwhile thing, as it were, finally put to use. The cursive letters were written in brown ink, and there was a maroon seal on the back with an image of a weeping willow incused in the wax. It was beautiful and delicate and Kevin was careful not to crack it in two as he opened the letter. The paper crinkled pleasantly under his fingers like one of those reproduction documents sold at historical site gift shops.

It was a work of art, from the elegantly florid hand to the flawless linear execution and knife-sharp margins. More than anything, though, it was the clarity of the message that he most admired, the lucidity of a cadenced thought, measured and expressed one word at a time without any trace of modern impetuosity. There was no date at the top, only a salutation followed by a few lines and a closing signature, underscored with a lacy, symmetrical paragraph.

Dear Mr. Heartstone,

I wished to tell you that it was not my intention to frighten you that day in the cemetery, though I am aware that without question my appearance elicited such a reaction. Heretofore, we have decided against attempting contact, fearing an inimical response from your contemporaries. Yet after reading your journal—an infringement on your privacy for which I here belatedly ask your forgiveness—I have concluded that you are not only a man of character, but perhaps of the particular disposition requisite of one who might find himself sympathetic to our plight . . .

I implore you come to us at 1 Grey Lane and offer counsel as to whether or not it would be prudent to attempt further contact. I hope that I may trust in your discretion with regard to keeping our whereabouts secret. Please be assured no harm will come to you.

> *With warm regards,*
> *Jane Cardinal*

The delayed 72 finally pulled up as Kevin read the last line. He gingerly folded the letter and slid it back between the pages of his commonplace book, stuffed the book in his bag, and hurried out the door. He'd never heard of Grey Lane— apparently, neither had the driver, who gave him a blank look and a dismissive shake of the head when Kevin inquired.

He reread the letter three more times during the ride to the east side. *Jane.* Her name was Jane Cardinal—Jane, who had lived over a hundred and fifty years ago. She had read his journal and, consequently, Kevin realized it meant that she knew more about him than anyone. "A man of character," she'd called him—words that made Kevin blush slightly. They filled him with a renewed sense of self-worth. It made him feel as if he could enter her tomb now and walk right into that unfathomable black without trepidation.

*

The police barriers closing off the block and diverting traffic around the cemetery were visible well before the bus reached Treestone. Huge sheets of riot-grade board erected along the entire length of the wrought iron perimeter fence obstructed any view of the grounds within. Kevin saw several large surveillance cameras set up in the corners of the yard, all

73

pointing inside. Vans decked with aerial antennae and bearing news channel logos were parked nearby; the reporters, illuminated by high-wattage lights, jostled for prime broadcasting spots. The major outlets were camped near the great Gothic arched main entrance, now flanked by a pair of guards—each bearing an automatic weapon.

Kevin got off at the stop just before the detour and walked to the corner of Progress Avenue and East 70th, watching the commotion for a while along with a smattering of bystanders—local residents by the sound of it—muttering to one another in low, apprehensive voices. Most of them had already witnessed everything an ignored urban district had to offer: fires and murders and police brutality and not least, the protracted entropic decline of their community perpetrated. It seemed fitting, then, that when the media finally came to this part of town it was in the interest of the dead, not the living.

Another gathering of people stood on the side of the road adjacent to Kevin. From out of this cluster, a single girl strode, crossed Progress Avenue and the police barriers, and approached the guards, who until that moment had been still as stone sentinels. They came to life as if freed from some immobilizing enchantment, moving forward in tandem to impede her, guns raised, though not pointed at her. The news outlets came to life as well, drawn to the action like a moth to a light bulb. Kevin didn't recognize the girl right away, not until she glanced back with shock at the surrounding camera crews and he saw those pellucid blue eyes: it was the enigmatic Tryer from his history class. She was demanding entrance to the cemetery, saying something about a relative buried there and sighting city code RA577.0 (The Right of the Living in all matters concerning the Accessibility and Honoring of their Dead, October 1912). The guards ordered her to step back, and when she did not, they raised their guns in perfect synchronization and aimed them at her.

This triggered two responses: silence at the epicenter where the standoff was occurring, and shouts from the loose assemblages gathered around the perimeter. Tension was building fast, the situation rapidly escalating toward a grim conclusion. Heart pounding, Kevin moved without thinking, walking out past the crowd and the correspondents and cameramen and around the barrier. As soon as he crossed this line, one of the guns was on him; the guard wielding it barking "Stop right there, put your hands up!" Kevin did as he was asked, but kept his focus on the girl. She had turned slightly to look at him; to his disappointment, he saw no sign of recognition in her eyes. Behind him, he could hear the reporters prattling in hushed though excited tones about this recent development. Everyone else had gone silent.

"Hey, come on," Kevin said to her, surprised at how composed he sounded. Outwardly he trembled uncontrollably. The girl didn't move, only stood there, continuing to stare at him with that bewildered expression.

"Come on, let's go," Kevin said with a sideways tick of the head. This time she blinked, then gazed around as if she'd been asleep and had suddenly woken in this taught as a tripwire situation. Her eyes returned to Kevin, who urged her on with a quick smile and another little wave. Slowly, she took a step backwards in his direction, followed by a second step, then a third. When she was in reach, he grabbed her hand and led her back through the barrier. As soon as they were clear, they ran instinctively, hand in hand, while the guards and reporters and onlookers stood there gawping as they fled. A moment later the spell broke, and the camera crews were chasing them, desperate to put names to the faces that would replay over and over again that night on every news outlet in the state.

As soon as they were clear of the crowds, the girl shook out of his grip and turned down an alley. At first he thought she was abandoning him to the pack of news anchors in pursuit. Then she reached out, grabbed his coat and hissed: *"This way."*

Together they pounded down the fractured brick passage between vine-ensnared garages and the graffitied backs of empty apartment buildings. At a break in a collapsing backyard fence, the girl dropped to her hands and knees and crawled through; Kevin followed. They sprinted across a rambling patch of overgrown yard littered with appliance carcasses and hills of black trash bags, then through the backdoor of a half-burned house.

Stepping through the wreckage—scorched paneling, clots of sodden newspaper, eviscerated furniture—they made their way into the mostly dark living room. The only light came from gaps where wooden planks nailed over the windows had warped or had been torn back the casings. They stood in the silence, hearts hammering, ears humming with the sound of their own rushing blood. "Do you hear anything?" Kevin asked, turning to the girl. She was glaring at him, fists balled at her sides, eyes stormy blue in the gloom. She shoved him without warning, sending him skittering backwards into a radiator. Kevin fell on his side, his elbow chafed and his left hip bruised.

"What the *hell?*"

"What the hell is right," the girl said, approaching him. Kevin raised an arm in defense.

"Why'd you push me?"

"Because you're an idiot. Who do you think you are?"

Kevin frowned. "Don't you recognize me?"

"Yeah, I recognize you. What does that got to do with anything?"

"Well, I'm sorry," Kevin said, getting to his feet. "I was just trying to keep *you* from getting shot."

The girl opened her mouth to speak, then closed it again. Kevin saw the crease in her brow relax. For a while they stood in awkward silence, until Kevin said: "So . . . who were you going to visit?"

"John Ellis Rodney," the girl said, peeking through a fracture in one of the window seals overlooking the backyard.

"The politician?"

"You know about him?"

"Of course. He was the first black man from this state

76

to be elected to the senate."

"He was also my great-great-great-great-grandfather."

"You hail from noble blood."

The girl eyed him curiously.

"I'm Kevin Heartstone," he said, offering his hand. The girl shook it.

"Coletta Hughes. You're very formal, Mr. Heartstone."

Kevin blushed and looked down at his shoes. "Do you live in this neighborhood?"

"A few blocks over, on Eloise. My family's been here for seventy-five years. They've got no right keeping us out of that cemetery. This whole city's turning into a military state." She appeared on the verge of tears—overly disappointed, Kevin thought, considering that she'd been on her way to visit an ancestor dead a century and a half. He thought he had an idea of what she'd been hoping to find at Treestone that afternoon—perhaps the same thing he had.

"What do you mean 'a military state'?"

"Haven't you heard? They're setting up checkpoints along the highways and doubling the number of active police on the streets, all to contain this . . . hoax, or whatever this is." She stepped away from the window. "They're lying to us. Nothing new about that though, especially around here."

"It's not a hoax," Kevin said. He drew the letter out of his bag and held it out. "One of them left this for me."

Coletta looked down at the parchment. "One of . . . *them?*"

"They're real. And Preventative Solutions has something to do with them coming back."

"Come *on,* man . . ."

"I'm serious! I was in Treestone two weeks ago and left my bag there. Today I wake up and it's sitting on my dining-room table with this note inside."

"And you think that a dead person returned it to you."

Kevin offered the letter again. "Read it for yourself."

Coletta smirked. "Look, thanks for ... doing whatever you did back there. But I'm gonna go." She stepped around him and started down the hall.

"You think I'm lying? By the way, what I 'did back there' was *save your life!*" he called after her as she tromped through the wreckage and disappeared through the hole in the fence without looking back.

Kevin receded into the hall, kicking at some brittle newspaper. He stood for a moment looking around at the ruined house. It made him feel sad. The place was drenched with sadness—from the filthy olive shag carpet sprawling like a polluted sea throughout the first floor to the daisy print border peeling along the ceiling in the scorched kitchen. These decorative preferences had been choices made by the house's occupants—reflections of their tastes as well as the vernacular style of their time. This had once been a home, a sanctuary, closed off from the elements and the eyes of the outside world—a private place, seasoned by hands and voices and body oils and bodily secretions and the millions of particles of dead skin that had settled over everything. It was a confluence of sights and smells and tactile remnants, singular as a fingerprint. A house like this had its own identity, unique as any human individual. Or, perhaps better said, since it had literally absorbed the physical traces of its owners, the structure was in some corporeal aspect a relic of a particular family's molted past—a shell that would never, not at least in the way it once had, live again. In order to bring it back, all remnants of What Was would have to be swept away, scrubbed, stripped, sledge hammered, sanctioned off, and sacrificed until it was bare and mute, returned to what it had been before those sacred inner spaces—those mini-universes in which entire lifetimes had played out—had been established. To realize that the entire city was filled with similar houses, thousands upon thousands of them, block after block, entire grids of demarcated plots burdened with the humiliating stigma of their unburied dead, was overwhelming. As Kevin thought all this, it seemed no wonder that the prevailing mood of Still City, not to mention his own emotional default setting, was generally and sometimes overbearingly morose. It was like living in a graveyard, a neglected one to boot, where the city's indifference was on perpetual display in the form of the moldering fabrications of their forefathers, the foundering templates of their departed passions and dreams.

He looked down at his name written on the parchment, and all at once he realized exactly what it was that he was holding: an invitation to confer with those very ancestors. An opportunity, perhaps, to obtain a decisive answer to the question that perennially loomed in the human psyche; the question that, as Emily Dickinson wrote, "worries one like a wasp." And they had chosen him; they'd decided he was "of the particular disposition," that *he* would understand them.

Pulling his hood up, Kevin stepped through the clutter, walked out the front door, and started up the road. A sharp winter draft coursed above the cratered pavement, lifting shingles and rattling loose siding panels on the deserted homes. He thought about his mother, wondering what she would think as the hours ticked by without him coming home. Would she send the police out looking for him? Would she have them lock him up in juvenile detention? He decided it didn't matter. Frank Heartstone's death had cleaved the family in two. His mother had chosen one path, the one with Chaz. Kevin, loyal to his father, chose the other—the one that led to Answers. *His* quest was bigger than everything— bigger, even, than whatever love remained in him for his mother.

The road ended at Commerce, the avenue that ran parallel to Progress. On the far side of the street, standing at the edge of the sidewalk between a ramshackle tire mechanic's and a windowless pink building with a neon sign reading "Peek-A-Boob," was a bus stop with a street map pressed behind a sheet of graffiti-tagged Plexiglas. Kevin scanned the index for Grey Lane. Alas, there was Granger and Grossman, but no Grey. Was the address Jane had given him some form of code? He supposed it was possible, but what would be the point? There was a particular urgency to her letter tha suggested she had no intention wasting time with riddles. Then it occurred to him that perhaps she was giving him the location as *she* remembered it—as it once was called.

Of course, Kevin thought, *the street has changed names.* It was common enough for a city that had grown from a commercial fishing port to major industrial metropolis. It made sense, but it didn't help him much. There was no way of finding it now, not without a visit to the city's Public Records department.

Then he thought: *If the lane is still there, and she's referring to an old address, the place she's at must be one that was there when she was alive . . .*

In his mind he began sifting through Still City's few extant nineteenth-century buildings, particularly ones that might have some reference to the color gray. Almost immediately he came up with it: *Halloween House.*

This wasn't the actual name of the place, but it was what Still City's youth had called it for generations. Why? Because the rundown Second Empire mansion with its mansard roof, stencil-like cresting, and imposing central tower was the stuff of gate groaning, werewolf howling, owl on a bare tree branch before the full moon with lightning striking and rain lashing terror that was every kid's—even Kevin's, who'd learned early on that houses themselves were nothing to be scared of—worst nightmare; i.e., finding himself or herself alone in the place at midnight on Halloween. And it had retained its fear quotient well into these same kids' adolescences, though the dread had curiously become altered. Teenagers dared one another to break in and steal a pruinose artifact—a pince-nez or a crystal demitasse or a candle snuffer, and so on, which had lain in situ for over a century. The really "brave" individuals claimed to have stayed the night in the house, gotten drunk in the formal dining room, and felt up their girlfriends on the parlor's camelback sofa, though the truth was that after swigging their gas station wine, each of them had slunk back out the same way they'd busted in long before the sun rose.

They had been afraid of the place as kids for one set of reasons. Now they were equally, if not more fearful, of a new set, which was somehow much more frightening than the former. It turned out that the place wasn't scary because of any of the things they'd expected to see or hear there, but because of the things they hadn't. Ghosts of any form would have been preferable to the unnerving, utter stillness—that eerie, soul-shadowing tomb silence, leaden and dense and without end, that they'd encountered within. Like total black, it seemed to absorb their light; it snuffed out their voices and moans, stifled their juvenile fervor and libidos until slowly they realized their eyes would never adjust to that dark because it was the color of Forever—a place beyond even their dreams of propitious Futures—which as youths was always coming, up and up, never seeming to arrive. Yet this house, full of that loaded Nothing, suggested that it *would* come—come to pass in fact.

Kevin himself had never entered Greysworth mansion, just as he'd never drank a sip of booze or kissed a girl. But unlike these latter rights of passage, he knew all about the infamous house.

It had been built for Winston Witney-Grey, who at fifteen immigrated to what was then known as DeStill City. He spent twelve years as a blacksmith's apprentice before serendipitously meeting Miles Russell, whose nascent Russell General Steel Co. had recently opened its first iron ore refinery along the south bank of the Kiksuyapi. Winston had no formal education or business training, but he was shrewd and ambitious and after only six months' work as a general laborer was promoted to foreman. Twenty years on found him RG Steel's vice president, and consequently one of the most powerful and affluent men in the nation.

He married the scandalously young Pamela Brecker

(eighteen years to his forty-nine) in 1859, had a daughter, Clementine, and built the rambling French-influenced sixteen-room mansion on the bluff near Fox Beach. The family lived in the house for less than a decade. Clementine disappeared when she was seven; supposedly she drowned in the lake, though her body was never found. Less than a year after, her father suffered a massive stroke in his office and died hours later at home. Though his wife was the predominant beneficiary of the estate, Witney-Grey had included a curious stipulation in his will concerning Greysworth. Though Pamela would inherit the mansion along with the bulk of her husband's wealth, neither she nor any of the house's subsequent inheritors were allowed to alter it or sell any of the furnishings or personal belongings for one hundred years after his death. To pay for this, he'd provisioned a large part of his fortune to care for and pay the taxes on Greyworth and the surrounding half-wooded three-acre parcel. It seemed that Winston never believed his daughter was really dead, and that if she returned, he wanted the house to remain as it was during those brief, happy times they'd passed together there.

Clementine, however, never came back.

Her grieving mother remained in the house only six months after Winston's death. A young widow, barely twenty-seven, Pamela had no intention of spending the rest of her life in a house of phantoms. She remarried, left all her things behind when she moved out (even her clothing), and never returned.

When Witney-Grey's bequest was depleted in 1968, the Still City Historical Society stepped in. For the next decade they managed to raise the necessary maintenance funds through tours, rentals, events, and private donors, though the majority of the capital was obtained from a preservation stipend funded by the state government. Budget cuts eliminated the endowment in 1983, forcing what little money the S.C.H.S. was able to elicit independently to be allocated to the most essential needs: exterior maintenance, grounds keeping, and security. Gradually, as both institutional and private interest in the house ebbed, so did the monetary allotments. By the late '90s, round-the-clock security declined to the occasional police drive-by, and eventually a flimsy and impotent NO TRESPASSING sign spanning the width of the dead-end road. Care of the property was reduced to once-a-season mowing.

Left vulnerable to the elements and the whims of vandals, Greysworth rapidly went into decline. Its contents were looted, its interior and exterior decayed. Despite this, the house retained a quiet dignity, perched on its lakeview rise, its central tower peeking through the treetops like a beacon. In the early 2000s, the windows were sealed to discourage further break-ins. The burglaries tapered off, and the remaining possessions, considerable in amount despite the pillaging, remained as they always had, sentinel-like, waiting for an age to return that would never come.

Yet now, apparently, it had. And Kevin himself had been summoned to join them—an ambassador to bridge the centuries—to offer counsel.

Yes, but they're dead . . . he thought. He flashed on the figures he'd glimpsed behind the Treestone gate, all those ragged suits and wilted bonnets. Eager as he was, he was also afraid, and wished that he had been able to convince Coletta to come with him. But she thought he was a fool, didn't she? Just like everyone else. A fool for guarding and advocating for the past and what "should" be left to rot. No, this would be his journey. He would answer their call. He would remain loyal to what had always taken precedence over everything else in his life: memory.

When the next bus heading west lumbered up to the stop, Kevin got on without hesitating.

4

Late that same evening, John Prise stood at one of the long rectangular windows in the half-renovated observation gallery

83

that occupied the fiftieth floor of Link Tower. He'd been standing there since an hour before sunset, watching the traffic crawl through the darkened streets of downtown, first a few headlights at a time, then a steady serpentine stream like a motorcade. This was once one of the most celebrated vantage points in the nation; a place from which one could view not only the swarming bustle of people in Central Square and the slick silver and black automobiles gliding along the avenues of storefronts with their newly installed neon signage, but the forested suburbs to the south and the west, and to the north, the endless columns of smoke from the mills, plants, and refineries darkening the layer of stratocumulus hovering over the blue diamond expanse of Lake Ahkohton.

Now, most of the windows were veiled in long black dropcloths to protect the glass from paint and sawdust and chips of flying stone as the restoration experts laboriously returned the pilastered rotunda, with its parquet floor and mosaic ceiling, to its former grandeur. Eventually the shrouds would come down, though the view would never be the same. The seventy-floor twin black monoliths known collectively as the Resurgence Centre (Resurgence being the largest power company in the region) and the Freedom Bank building (which, at eighty stories, now held the distinction as tallest in the state) obscured the formerly unobstructed vista on three sides. Each of these modern edifices had their own observation levels, yet none equaled the elegance of the "City's Compass," as the Link deck came to be known, nor did they overtake (though their architects had tried) the Tower as symbolic icon. Link was and always would be, diminutive in comparison though it was, the star of the skyline, the city's lodestar.

Fifty years had passed since the Central-Link Railroad Co. had abandoned the Still City main station and its hundred or so offices for smaller headquarters in a minor city one state over. The structure itself was in need of some critical repairs and interior renewal. Touring the complex and tower was a walk through time. Beneath the cheap wood paneling, drop ceilings, and pale green industrial carpeting was a wealth of Art Deco and Beaux-Arts detail. Built of local limestone and white granite, there was a fairytale-like aspect to the tower, especially when the pennant-style state flag hanging from its pinnacle caught the wind. The exterior, dulled and dirtied by fifty years of smoke and automobile exhaust, was cleaned and the interior restored, including the great vaulted lobby (transformed into a shopping arcade) and twenty-five of its lower floors, which had been converted into high-end apartments. The remaining floors (various office spaces), the old Banner Grill, and the observation deck were still under renovation. John Prise had brought it back, stripping away the modern mass-produced materials to reveal the beauty hidden at the foundation; for in those eloquent features was not only a treasure of forgotten art, but a city's pride and identity.

It was Prise's love of antiquity as well as his city that motivated him. He'd double majored in history and poli-sci as an undergraduate, and his master's thesis had concerned the historical implications of urban and regional planning of the greater Still City area, with a focus on social and economic mobility. It had prepared him for his rise through local government, first as a city councilor (at twenty-six, the youngest in SC's history) for three terms, then deputy mayor for the former administration, before running in his own contested election, which he'd won by a hair.

Resurrecting Link Tower—making it viable again— had restored some of that aforementioned pride. In the four years since securing National Landmark status, the tower had enjoyed almost constant media attention, and thus attracted a score of both local and corporate business as well as legal and financial institutions, all eager to fill space in a rejuvenating urban center. This, combined with an emerging interest in reclamation of the area neighborhoods and the largely vacant downtown, had spurred and unexpected rebirth—a celebration of all things Still City—and John Prise had been at the helm of it all. T-shirts and flags and hats started appearing with slogans like "I STILL Believe," "SC the Future," and "STILL the Best"—each including an image of Link Tower incorporated either in the Ls or Ts. Coincidentally, the perennial loser professional sports teams had suddenly leapt into relevance: the Blasters had made it to basketball's Eastern Conference Finals and the Spiders had actually won the World Series two months earlier. And though the greater metro area remained a residential and industrial graveyard, there was a pulse at the city's nucleus that grew a little louder each day.

All this filled Prise with both civil and personal gratification. True, the shift toward reconstruction began during the years leading up to his first term, but he had been the one to accelerate it to an unprecedented level. His declaring a state of emergency in his first days in office immediately provided fodder for his detractors, who'd labeled him a reactionary promising grandiose things he couldn't deliver. But in fact the move had accomplished exactly what the new mayor had hoped. It had gotten everyone's attention, showed them that he was aware of the city's major issues, and that he wasn't going to promulgate progress based solely on one or two percentage points of improvement in the unemployment crate, nor pretend that Still City was truly represented in those strategically taken photos posted by the tourism board that sought to highlight the few picturesque views—always adjacent to (though careful not to include) ruin. He'd rolled his figurative sleeves up and was ready to dig into the city's issues with the same vigor his Eastern European grandfathers had with their shovels and pickaxes when they carved out the modern municipal foundation. He'd inherited their resilience and perseverance along with their dark eyes and thickset builds; he was a native of this place, bred here, invested in the cause both ancestrally as well as spiritually. Which made what he had just done so ironically tragic.

An hour ago, he had held a televised press conference

during which he confirmed the seemingly implausible rumors and reports: the dead were in fact walking the streets. For this, he had publicly blamed Preventative Solutions. It had been so-called political suicide, and he knew that the imbroglio that followed would without doubt lead to his removal from office. But his own future with regard to politics no longer mattered to him. The damage was done: *he* had opened Pandora's Box by spearheading PS's arrival, *he* (with the city council's approval) accepted their massive contribution to aid in restoring Link Tower (on the irritating condition that it be renamed "Link Tower at PS Point"), and thus, *he* was to blame for what would certainly come to be known as the worst ecological disaster in modern history. Dead people, reanimated by toxic runoff, walking around downtown. It was horror novel drivel, but this wasn't some pulp rag full of clichéd zombies. It was going on in his city, amidst all the hard-earned progress and revitalization efforts, and it was his fault.

But John wouldn't be a puppet. He wouldn't lie about what was going on to protect the devious interests of Preventative Solutions or the reputation of a rogue like Serge Vexivus. John Prise had one more political battle to wage, and he would fight with every ounce of his pugnacious, dogged resolve.

For now though, he only wanted to stand in the peace and the silence, here at this apex, and watch the rind of sun disappearing west of the city he loved. As he gazed at that fading light, a Marcus Aurelius aphorism came to him: *Let nothing interfere with doing what is right.* Yes, he decided, what he had done was right. Weighed in his conscience he found it, as if against Maat's feather, balanced.

A sound (a door closing?) interrupted his tranquility. He'd told his guards not to disturb him until he'd called for them. Perhaps there was an emergency? Cocking his head toward the door, he waited for a knock, but none came. He turned back to the window, then spun around when he heard the click. It took a second or two to process the open door, and the dark outline of a man standing before one of the long black dropcloths. The man's face was expressionless. A beam of sun winked off the silencer of his gun. There was an audible chirp; the mayor sank to the glossy polished floor, and on that window facing west, a volcanic spray brilliant as brimming lava spattered, superimposed against the red and orange shell burst of twilight.

III.

.

". . . and what if thou withdraw
In silence from the living, and no friend
Take note of thy departure?"

WILLIAM CULLEN BRYANT

1

It was a curse unto the Land; like a boil, ever festering, ever oozing, seeping, secreting its multifarious poisons. The soil was weary and defenseless. Its only power was regeneration, and since the spilling and dumping and emptying never stopped, the Land never healed. For two hundred years it bore its affliction like a beast of burden. It stagnated and sank beneath the contemptible weight of brick, wood, stone, steel, and the millions of unyielding creatures who perpetually hacked and hammered at their seething creation— demolishing it, rebuilding it, sacrificing themselves to it.

It hadn't always been like this. For an eon there had only been the Land itself, continuously shifting and re-forming, but elementally remaining the same. The mud broiled like flesh during sultry eras and dried to an arid exoskeleton under glacial advance. Beneath this indomitable sheet it slept for an age, loaded with dormant seed dreaming of thaw. The current waterways were formed around ten or so millennia ago when the ice melted, followed soon after by the first of the Infestation.

These initial inhabitants were nothing like the latter; they were placid and gentle, reverential of the Land, humbled by it. They comprehended their own transience, both in place and time, and the "roots" they put down went only as deep as their tent stakes. Sometimes they stayed—set up communities, built fires, made their noises, hunted and gathered food— though never for long. When one of them died, the others gouged a pocket into the terra firma and inserted the body. The Land slowly digested these, returning them to carbons and chemicals; these it redistributed, leaving behind, like the peripatetics themselves, no trace.

The man (eponym of the infestation incarnate) and his party came after his own people's removal of the prior race. He stood on a rise overlooking the swampy lowlands, surveying what lay before him like a lord. His step was not like the others; it was deliberate and calculating. His men drew lines, defined boundaries. They leveled the mounds containing the remaining bones of the placid people and shoveled them into the tortuous river. Those initial years were full of comings and goings, and every time they returned, this new lot brought with them more of everything: materials, animals, and not least, more like themselves. They spread like choke weed over the Land. They put it under their yoke like their broken livestock. They dammed the river, both literally and figuratively, with boards and with waste. They felled the trees and used them as fuel for their industrious fires. Smoke roiled in black, sun-blotting curtains. But this was a mere irritation compared to the noxious triumvirate of sewage, toxic runoff, and barrel upon barrel of sludgy byproduct tunneled through the loam like poisoned roots.

The river, the principal vessel that drained and purified the Land, flowed like a clogged artery toward its delta. No fish swam in its channel. Nothing grew along its riparian zone. Not even the pestilent denizens themselves dared venture into it, lest they be devoured by their own personal and manufactured excrement. In a relatively short while, things began to happen that shouldn't—paradoxical anomalies such as burning water, caustic rain fatal to vegetation, and most aberrant of all, the interred rising from the ground. For generations they had lain preserved like sap-captured mosquitoes in the manufactured soup the saturated Land and air couldn't process. When they resurfaced they were like things raised from an impossibly deep and inaccessible shipwreck; things that were never meant to be seen or touched or even thought of again.

The Land was too sick and subjugated to resist. It had become a mere foundation—trampled, bitter bedrock, hard and harvestless as the hundreds of thousands of tons of reinforced concrete heaped upon on its back. Now, tainted and barren of stock, the Land slept as if on life support, without dreams, without hope for liberation, without the promise of a thaw.

2

Jenna Heartstone suffered from "nerves"—a condition she had self-diagnosed herself with after her husband's death. She remembered her mother telling her that Jenna's great-grandmother had suffered from the same: "nerves" being the catch-all term for numerous classifications of contemporary mental illnesses and disorders including but not limited to depression, anxiety, bipolar, schizophrenia, OCD, and PTSD. To a pharmaceutical engineer it sounded ridiculously old-fashioned—on par with people who had "spells." Whatever the case, it was clear to Jenna that she was suffering. Besides her scattered thoughts (she often stuttered or rambled when trying to express them), her random and excessive laughter at inappropriate situations, and her manic bouts of weeping, there was a bevy of physical identifiers: nails bit low, hair thinning, skin gray as unprimed canvas in the dim living room where she sat, shades drawn against the waning winter sun, a hint of halitosis lurking on the air. She'd lost twenty-one pounds, and would have shed more if it weren't for the wine. She didn't wear shorts or short-sleeved shirts because she hated the knobbiness of her elbows and knees. The flesh of her face had receded, making her teeth protrude and her eyes bulge slightly so that she appeared vaguely skeletal in the television light.

She was staring at a rerun of a sitcom she and Frank used to watch before Kevin was born, in the days when the house was still unfinished and it seemed as though it would always be. It was disquieting seeing how the styles contrasted between the characters on the show and the people in the intervening commercials. How quickly everything changed, became *past*. This had been the reason for the argument with Chaz. She hadn't felt like going to brunch earlier, hadn't felt like doing much of anything actually since the night of Kevin's confession in the foyer. When she'd brought up her dead husband in relation to the TV show, it had been the proverbial straw and camel analogy for Chaz on the subject.

He'd reached for the remote, turned off the television, and told her they needed to talk.

"I thought you said you were over this," Chaz had said.

"*Over* what?" Jenna replied darkly.

"Not over it. I mean, you know … processed it … moved on from Frank," he'd replied, then mumbled: "I'll tell you what, your son sure hasn't." He'd stood up and started pacing in the spot the Christmas tree typically occupied. Suddenly it occurred to her that it was Christmas week. Why hadn't they gotten a tree? And where *was* Kevin? It was three in the afternoon, and she hadn't seen or heard him all day. Motherly instinct seized her suddenly with reptilian alertness. Her eyebrows ticked down as she looked at the glass of wine in her hand—her second within the hour—and then at Chaz. It was like being snapped out of a spell.

"I think you should leave."

"Jenna, I didn't mean—"

"I have some things I need to take care of. To think through …" She paused, then added: "I'll call you, okay?"

Chaz stood, arms akimbo. "That sounds like a bad break-up line."

"It's not. I promise."

"Well, take all the time you need. Maybe I'll wait for that call, and maybe I won't," he'd said. He slammed the door as he left, letting slip some carefully repressed anger.

Jenna closed her eyes, huffed, shook her head. Not for the first time she recognized how ridiculous the relationship was, and yet she continued to try, to contort and constrain and transmute herself in order to fit the role he expected. She knew that she would call him later and apologize, even though on a gut level she didn't want to, didn't feel it was her responsibility to. Why, then, did she continue to endure and entertain it, prolong this imprudent attempt at again "finding love"? She knew she'd let it go on in part because Chaz was, in every way possible, the opposite of Frank. There was his taste in art (essentially non-existent unless it concerned the variations in Still City's sports franchises' logos throughout history); his attitude toward his work (profit over preservation); his propensity for treating sex as a job to be done—machine-like, an automaton devoid of intuiting even the vaguest erotic innuendo. Yet she was also attracted to his pragmatism and unsentimental nature and to the way he was guided as if by some optimistic inner compass leading him, *ergo* her, *forward* rather than backward. But had she really committed herself, either to Chaz or the notion of permanently (at least in a relationship sense) moving on from her husband? Maybe he was right: maybe she wasn't "over" Frank, but it wasn't her fault. There was no eluding what was omnipresent every single morning, afternoon, evening, night. There was the house, which hadn't changed in four years and was beginning to feel like a paused film frame; there was her son, who lurked around solemn and stone-faced as a monk, guarding the sacred flame of his father's memory; there was the room at the back of the house, to enter which was like abrading a wound. Finally, there was her grief, unrelenting and unrestrained as a cold wind coursing over a dead, treeless plain.

Jenna had always excelled in math and science, not metaphysics. Her métier had been fact, careful study, and trial. She didn't "do" counseling; she combined chemicals that altered other chemicals, and she trusted her own work above all else, especially during the great crisis of her life. She believed in Plaiscene and in her team. She'd continued going to work, never taking a bereavement day, never turning to the church or religion—her only "faith" being that old axiom that work was the only relief from rooted sorrow—and in the evenings, she took her pill along with the rest of the nation, righteously convinced of its power to relieve.

So didn't that make her pragmatic too? Perhaps she had more in common with Chaz on an innate level than she wanted to admit. She'd unabashedly stood by her employer through the weeks of recent scandal, even though she was egregiously underpaid (considering the billions PS leeched annually from insurance companies, Mederal—the federal low income aid program—and the millions of individuals and families paying out of pocket); even though she felt a dark flutter in her chest with each new report of the city-wide hoax that was turning out to be something . . . else.

Jenna knew that unadulterated plecebala was exceedingly unstable. Lab experiments on rats had shown increased docility once the proper dosage had been determined. But the tests leading up to this had been much more fascinating, albeit frightening, particularly when the early subjects who had died from high dosing continued, miraculously, to show stabilized brain activity despite the fact that the animals were no longer breathing and their hearts had stopped—in some cases, as much as *seven days* later. Some had even opened their eyes and crawled into the corners of the clear test containers from which, still as stuffed animals, they eerily observed their observers. These "side effects," as PS called them, were still being furtively assessed. Jenna had been privately relieved when the EPA recently instituted regulations that the excess plecebala be filtered from the water used to process it before sending it for further treatment, though she was beginning to wonder whether PS was bypassing this step. It would explain the mayor's recent visit to the facility, as well as his surprise drop-in at the house last month for the first time since the weeks after Frank's death.

Idly sipping her wine, Jenna replayed the meeting in her head. They'd sat in this very room, drinking coffee, John nervously rolling the cup between his thick fingers and gazing around the house as if he expected to see Frank's ghost drifting along the crown molding. He had come alone—no guards, no retinue. Just "old friends catching up," he'd said. And then he'd begun asking big questions about PS and Plaiscene, complex and specific inquiries that Jenna quickly became uncomfortable answering. Still, she had told him the truth; told him about plecebala and how it worked and about her concerns regarding its disposal. John listened without interrupting, his face set in a practiced politician's mask.

After this rather stiff conversation, he'd suddenly and awkwardly invited her to dinner. Jenna knew that John had been in love with her since the day they'd met in freshman year organic chemistry. John had dropped the class within a week, though not before asking her out. They'd gone for pizza. There were no fireworks for Jenna, though the same couldn't be said later when they ran into John's roommate on the way back to campus. Jenna had started seeing Frank soon after. For John, it had been another burr between friends— and yet another victory for Frank, who always seemed to win life's coin toss in everything from girls to grants. Not that things became bitter or vengeful between them, but Jenna had been the first fathom of a deepening gulf between good friends. She supposed declining John's dinner offer had been the reason for the cold, overly formal look he'd given her as he passed her in the hall at PSHQ a few days back. But she wondered whether their casual meeting in her parlor held more significance than John led on. Did he suspect that she was lying in the hopes of extenuating the scandal and PS's responsibility for it?

She glanced at the window. The antique panes were already washed with sunset color. She realized it was the 21th—the solstice, and only four days from Christmas. She looked again at the place where the tree should be, and wondered what Frank would say if he saw her now— wrapped in a musty fleece in the rapidly darkening room, drinking through a hangover and with no idea where Kevin was. The sitcom credits rolled on the TV screen, followed by the headlines for the upcoming 5 o'clock news. Jenna, watching but only half watching, didn't at once recognize the boy standing with his hands raised and guns pointed at him. She didn't recognize the girl either for that matter, or the setting with all the bright lights and news crews surrounding it. As one of the cameras zoomed in on the boy Jenna sat up, blindly placing the wine glass on the edge of the table next to her. She didn't react as the glass crashed onto the floor, the dregs within flying like blood spatter.

It *was* Kevin—with two automatic weapons aimed at his chest; Kevin beckoning some girl, as if she were standing on a bridge and about to jump. Jenna watched the girl step forward, take his hand, watched them run away together pursued by the news anchors and camera crews. Her hand shook as she grasped the remote control, turned up the volume. *Unidentified teenagers outside Treestone Cemetery,* they were calling them—unidentified, as if they were dead bodies pulled from the river.

Jenna suddenly snapped to, disentangled herself from the throw blanket, and stood—too fast; the afternoon's three glasses of wine rushed to her brain. She rested a palm on her forehead, closed her eyes, then opened them again. There was broken glass on the floor. She frowned. *When did that happen?* She got a broom and dustpan from the kitchen. *Goddammit, he went there again,* she thought as she swept up the mess. "Willfully disobeyed me," she said, sweeping harder, shards flying past the pan. She carried what she'd gathered into the kitchen, dumped it into the trash, then threw broom and dustpan into the closet and kicked the door shut. *I'm putting a deadbolt on the outside of his door. But first, I'm going to take all his goddammed books, so he'll have nothing to do but think of what an arrogant, ungrateful little shit he is . . .*

She marched upstairs, her rage mounting as she changed clothes, choosing a sweater, then tearing it off and firing it across the room. She did the same with a pair of jeans, a turtleneck, tennis shoes—before finally settling on some khakis and a hooded sweatshirt. Downstairs she grabbed her coat and keys, slamming the front door as she left. She stuck the key in the ignition of her pale blue sedan, gunned the engine in reverse, and tore out of the driveway, heading in the direction of the Interstate.

A dark gray SUV pulled out behind her, high beams on, riding her close. Jenna flipped her rearview mirror, dimming the headlights, and pressed the gas pedal, shifting hard. She was already fifteen miles over the speed limit, but the SUV rode her close. She threw a black look at the mirror, and the SUV backed off a bit as she started up the highway ramp. Up ahead the lane, hedged by a concrete parapet, tapered as it merged left onto Interstate 31. Jenna put her turn signal on, started to move over, but jerked the wheel back when she saw the SUV suddenly on her left, matching her speed. The lane was narrowing quickly, with nowhere for her to go. Jenna glanced frantically at the SUV's tinted windows, black and inscrutable as arachnid eyes. She beeped the horn, slowed, and tried to slip in behind it, but the SUV kept pace. The wall loomed—twenty, ten yards away. Shrieking, Jenna slammed on the brakes. The last thing she was aware of was the anti-lock system kicking in a moment before the passenger-side headlight smashed into the low concrete wall, sending the sedan's rear end jutting out into traffic where it collided with another car before skidding to a stop across two lanes, facing in the opposite direction.

The dark gray SUV slid, unseen, into the far left lane and accelerated, heading east.

3

Grey Lane was a dead appendage off West Arbor Road—the main access way that ran through Fox Beach State Park. Two concrete barriers flanked the lane's entrance with a chain like a thin necklace strung between them. Dangling from this, by one rusty grommet, was a sign that read NO TRESPASSING ON THE ORDER OF STILL CITY PD. Kevin walked along the sand-strewn pavement, the lake on his right, an empty parking lot on his left. He could see Greysworth's mansard tower rising above the winter woods, its cresting rusted, its oculus window boarded and blind. He ducked under the flimsy chain, the NO TRESPASSING sign squawking crow-like as it swung. The lane was thick with dead weeds and forest scruff. There was a sizable deadfall that appeared to have lain undisturbed across the path for several seasons. It was a confirmation of the city's lack of interest in the property.

They'd sealed the house and let nature form its own blockade.

Kevin climbed over the rotting tree and then paused a few paces on the other side to gauge the direction of the lane, which was becoming more difficult to determine the further he walked. Saplings had sprouted everywhere, up through the mineral-rich carpet of dead leaves, blurring the road's boundaries. The fact that it was getting dark quickly added to his apprehension. Fear spread through him like spilled ink as he glanced up at the branch fingers raking deepening gray ceiling of cloud. It was ominous and eerily still and it reminded Kevin of where he was going, and whom he was going there to meet. He looked over his shoulder at the black hulking deadfall lying like a discarded body. Beyond it, the road wound back to the beach and the relentless surf, to the grimy bus stop and the dirty glow of the city. Noise and lights and life and the reinforcing certainty that went along with them. Ahead lay the indeterminate; a vague path he'd have to find his way through in the gloaming, every unknown sound amplified in his ears, each of his steps an invasion of the established silence of a dominion of decay. And yet, wasn't this the direction he'd been heading for the past four years?

He continued through the brambles, following a tamped-down area in the brush that he took to be the edge of the road. The way was mostly uphill, though the incline was slight; still he could feel the burn in his thighs, knew that he was climbing. The lane terminated at two stone columns connected by an arcing gate covered in clumps of vine. The gate was shut, but not locked. Kevin peered through. The top of the bluff was two acres of calf-high yellow grass through which a continuation of the lane, narrower and paved with fine gravel, wound up to Greysworth's porch. There was only one tree on the entire property—an old gnarled cherry, standing beside the path like a leaning scarecrow. The house itself stood to the right of the gate on the apex of the hill, a great looming shipwreck of a place, its front door facing the city. For a long time Kevin just stared at it. The peeling façade was the color of shadows and dried tea. The porch spandrels were patterned like spiderwebs. Every window was boarded. He pictured the city crew coming with their particle board sheets and screw guns, the screws boring into the window caps and aprons, perforating the hand-carved woodwork. The damage was irreversible, but negligible compared to the other, more severe alterations it might have suffered. Essentially the house was untouched by contemporary hands. What it must be like inside! Kevin thought. And then he shuddered as he remembered that *they* were in there, gathered in the dark, waiting for him. How claustrophobic, how dim and dank, how—

Tomb-like.

A branch snapped behind him; the sound seemed loud as a gunshot in the silence. Kevin looked back—so fast he felt the muscles in his neck burn. He scanned the trees, expecting to see some half-decomposed face peering at him through the gloom. Nothing was there, though he thought he heard the sound of footsteps receding through the leaves.

Turning back to the gate, he lifted the rusted latch and pushed, the hinges squealing shrilly like some archaic alarm system. As he started up the lane, a man emerged from behind the dead cherry. He held out a lantern; the flame flickered, illuminating his wasted features, flat and cold despite the warmth of the light. The face was gray, with a trencher beard and concave cheeks. The thin lips were sucked so tightly against the teeth that Kevin could see the outline of the dead man's bite. The eyes, radioactive green, fixed on Kevin. The stench of foul mud mixed with something acerbic and faintly chemical wafted from him as he approached, his movements slow and plotted like a spider. His clothing was matted and soiled though the dirt appeared streaked, as if he'd tried to brush it off.

This is a corpse, Kevin thought. Its only duty was to decay, and yet: notice the man's bearing; his inclination, despite death, to maintain a semblance of fastidiousness and urbanity. It eased Kevin's fear, reminded him that there was an intellect within the desiccated shell standing before him. It also made him remember his manners. He straightened, cocking his head slightly upward, fixing his gaze on those unnerving green orbs.

"My name is Kevin Heartstone. I have come on the invitation of a Ms. Jane Cardinal."

The man regarded him, utterly still, so still he seemed like a prop from some hyper-realistic haunted house. *He's not breathing,* Kevin thought. And then: *no heartbeat either.* He wondered if the man could hear him, if that sensory ability had accompanied the body beyond the grave. Or perhaps he couldn't speak? Kevin tried to imagine what the man's tongue must look like. A piece of bark? Maybe he should show him the letter. As he reached for his bag, the man nodded and, without a word, turned and started toward the house. Kevin followed him at a distance, up the weathered front steps of the bracketed porch and over the threshold of Halloween House.

The foyer was low-lit by a series of candles on sconces mounted along the crimson damask walls. Kevin looked around, astounded: he was standing in a Victorian time capsule. Preserved, however, wasn't the term he would have used to describe it; *untouched* was more appropriate. There were cracks in the ceiling plaster, rodent prints in the dust, the strong fustiness of horsehair furniture. The walls were sooty from fireplace smoke and blotched with water stains. But there was also a luster to the oak moldings and the elegant turns of the staircase's newel post and balusters, rich detail in the pargeting of the ceiling, and a drowned shine to the grand chandelier. Kevin looked up the stairs, rising into blackness, pondering the treasures that filled the rooms above them—the abandoned personal effects of Winston Whitney-Grey and his family.

The man carried the lantern to a side table left of the stairs and set it down. On the table was a small glass decanter and a folded white towel. Kevin watched, simultaneously curious and anxious as the man unstoppered the bottle and poured a thin line of the fluid along the embroidered fabric, after which he replaced the glass bauble plug, picked the towel up and, with bowed head, offered it to Kevin. It smelled flowery sweet, like lilies or heliotrope. For several moments Kevin looked at the towel before finally comprehending. It was to mask the smell—*their* smell. Kevin accepted the cloth but as a return courtesy did not hold it to his face as the dead man took up the lantern again and led him into the drawing room. The lantern light disclosed magnificent glimpses of Rococo detail: chartreuse brocade, lacy antimacassars, the carved rosewood of a Belter sofa, the glint of gold ormolu. Candlelight glowed in the room beyond—the room where *they* were gathered, waiting for him.

The parlor was brighter than the other rooms, the space high-ceilinged, the walls papered twilight blue with an elaborate star/arrow pattern and the repeating image of a sheaf of wheat. There was a tarnished mirror in a faded silver frame above a marble mantle to Kevin's right. No fire burned in the fireplace. The dead were arranged like an audience, seated in musty armchairs and sofas, standing in the dim corners, flanking the doorways and the fireplace. They smelled not of rot, but like dried flowers or sun-spoiled fruit. Their clothing was flat and creased—brittle taffeta, stained silk and linen, disintegrated cotton and wool. Some wore fresh vêtements, perhaps the wardrobe of Mr. and Mrs. Whitney-Grey, preserved in those long-sealed chifforobes and closets. Others remained wrapped in their dwindled grave cerements. Small twin boys dressed in short pant suits gazed at Kevin from the bench of a piano—tibias and fibulas exposed, their bone fingers entwined. He could see the gaping cranial lines running along the tops of their fleshless heads. There was a man crouching alone in a corner, staring at his feet and mumbling to himself as if he were counting the bones of his toes. Kevin could tell by his rotted vestments that the man had been a priest. At the center of a room sat a dignified black man, his features gaunt and leathery as a bog mummy. A woman wearing a long white gown and a bonnet like a wilted daffodil stood before one of the sealed windows.

She held a baby whose face was mostly skull, milk teeth exposed along with the rest of its jaw. The baby regarded Kevin with eyes that were not flesh but soft luminous beams of bright green. They all had the eyes; they all peered at him like alien lights.

The man who had led Kevin in now stood at the center of the room beside a high-backed Baroque queen chair trimmed in black velvet. In the chair sat a remarkably preserved and regal dead man. His face was square and thin-lipped. He glared at Kevin with narrowed, deepset eyes. He wore a tombstone-style shirt, shawl collared vest, string tie, and black frock coat. His chestnut hair was thick, styled with a few swipes of macassar. A walking stick topped with a ruby orb rested casually against his inner thigh. Kevin realized that the others seemed to be waiting for this man to speak. Kevin reached in his bag, took out the letter from Jane, and held it up in the blush of taper light.

"My name is—"

"We know who you are and why you've come," said the man in the chair. His voice was surprisingly clear, with only a slight rasp—a baritone that Kevin supposed must have been stentorian in life. Kevin's own voice caught in his throat. He swallowed, coughed, pressed the back of his hand to his lips. He was trembling. He tried to think of something to say, but his mind was as dry as his mouth. Despite Jane's reassurances, he seemed not at all welcome. He scanned the room but did not see her. "I was told you wish to speak to me. That you . . . seek counsel," he said.

"On the contrary, Mr. Heartstone, we demand *answers,*" the man in the chair replied. "Perhaps you were expecting an assemblage of wide-eyed grovelers, kneeling at the altar of modernity? We have seen *your* age—every insipid and vulgar detail."

"I despise it as much as you," Kevin replied bewilderedly.

"Why should we expect you to be any less its product?" said a man seated on the mayor's right. He had the

104

long face and steel wool beard of a late-Victorian president. They were all glaring at him now—a boy on the witness stand, made to argue posterity's case. Anger flared in Kevin. He crossed his arms, stared fixedly at the man in the chair.

"I won't pretend that I'm not of my time. But I will not allow you to accuse me of being responsible for it."

The man in the chair sat up slightly, took the ball of the walking stick in his right palm, and rested his left atop the former. "The response of a *man of his time* indeed," he said coldly.

"Please, Father, it is discourteous to berate our guest," a voice said plaintively. Kevin turned and saw the girl from the tomb emerge from the darkened drawing room. She had changed her dress; the one she wore now was flat gray and off-shoulder. Her hair was also different, parted in the middle, the ribbons gone and the dark tresses worked into shoulder-length corkscrew curls, but she still wore the black laced mitts and coral necklace. She clutched a small bunch of flowers bound with a thin white silk thread: ivory Christmas rose and winterberry holly along with a thatch of wild thyme. She handed these to Kevin, who accepted them awkwardly.

"Jane, come away from him this instant!" the man in chair said sharply.

"He is not a threat, Father. He has come to assist us."

"It seems to me his only concern is that of defending *himself*. You should have spoken with me before inviting him here. How shall we fare when he inevitably reveals our whereabouts?"

Several of the dead muttered in accord.

"He has no intention of doing so. It was a condition of his coming here, and I for one honor his word. Perhaps addressing him more genially would induce him to impart upon us some of his contemporary wisdom."

"I dare say you've just uttered an oxymoron, my dear," Jane's father said. He huffed impatiently. "Nevertheless, and against my better judgment, I will oblige you. Mr. Heartstone?" he said, and raised a hand, palm

105

upward, in the direction of the hearth where an empty chair stood. Kevin hesitated, then cautiously moved toward it and sat, the stares of the dead following him. Jane settled into an anthemion chair left of her father. Kevin shivered as his sat; it wasn't out of fear, but of thrill. He was sitting in their presence—the faces in the daguerreotypes and ambrotypes, the ferrotypes and cartes-de-visite. They were much altered of course, but authentic. They sat with the upright posture of the individuals in those photos, hands folded primly in their laps. In contrast, Kevin realized he was slouching. He scooched up, his back settling against the wooden dowels of the chair.

"May I ask your names?" Kevin said.

"The Honorable Elias J. Cardinal," Jane's father said.

"Silas Leeds, physician and eighteenth mayor of this city," said the man seated on the judge's right. The others were silent.

"They have names, to be sure, though most no longer have the ability to utter them," the black man said. Kevin looked at him, at his heavy eyebrows, the deep nasolabial furrows, the fixed recalcitrance in his expression. Yes, there was a picture of this man in Kevin's civics textbook. He was John Ellis Rodney, the first black senator from this state, and ancestor of Coletta Hughes.

"Several have elected to remain in their graves," Silas Leeds added.

"Of course, right . . ." Kevin stammered, though he hadn't considered this. He flashed on them, lying in their silent tombs, or worse, contained within their coffins, willfully buried alive. It made him break out in gooseflesh. He bit his lip, knowing the next question he wanted to ask. His eyes swept the figures in the room. "Do you know why you've come back?"

"We had hoped that you might be able to provide us with an explanation," said the judge.

"Actually, I do have a theory . . ."

Chatter and whispers broke out. With all eyes on him,

Kevin drew a deep breath and exhaled with a shudder. The room suddenly felt icy. His teeth began to chatter, and he couldn't seem to stop them. Never had he been so conscious of his vital forces and functions: the thrum of his pulse, the whoosh of blood in its circuitous pattern through his veins, the quivering muscle, one twitching eye, his breathing like roaring wind in the vacuum-like stillness. "There is a drug called Plaiscene that's being manufactured in the city. I believe what's happening to you has something to do with it."

"What is this drug utilized for?" Silas asked. "Is it an antipyretic?"

"I'm not familiar with that term. You mean like an antibiotic?" Kevin asked, then immediately felt foolish. Vaccines and immunization in their current form hadn't existed for these folk—not until the 1880s, followed two decades later by the modern "antibiotic era."

"Antipyretics are agents of fever reduction," Silas said. "And what of the remedies of which you speak?"

"A vaccine is a diluted dose of a live illness administered as an injection."

"Such as the one for cowpox," Silas interjected.

"Yes, but we have them for many diseases now: measles, chicken pox, diphtheria, flu, tuberculosis. We get most of them when we're kids. Antibiotics are different. They're used to treat bacterial infections."

"A cure for consumption has been discovered?" came a voice from the back of the room. It was faint and crackly, like a breeze passing through dead leaves. The speaker was a woman, wearing a plaid hoop skirt dress that was too big for her, and a tarnished cameo at her throat. A small child in a flounced red dress stood on the table beside her. At first Kevin thought it was a young girl, but then he saw that what remained of its web-thin hair was parted on the side, not down the center. There was something poignant in their staid postures, in their dejected countenances, in their recognition of a stone-solid truth that the great all-consuming specter of their age had been conquered. It was as if Kevin's admission was almost too much for them to bear—this tiny contingency of the vast multitude devoured by the White Death. A few cc's of liquid inoculum had put an end to its pernicious reign, but here in these phantom eyes the legacy of its devastation remained undiminished. Preserved along with them had been their suffering, their helplessness—all the agonies of this particular mother's unbearable loss.

"Yes," Kevin said, nodding sadly. "Plaiscene, however, isn't a cure for anything. It's what's known as an antidepressant."

"Antidepressant," Jane repeated. "Is that a treatment for melancholia?"

"No. Just general stress: job stress, social stress, relationship stress. 'Anxiety' is the term used today. It is a mood-altering substance. It's supposed to 'take the edge off.'"

Judge Cardinal scoffed. "What you are saying is that this 'medication' is required in order to perform life's *basic tasks?*"

"For the people who take it, yes," Kevin said, then quickly added: "But I'm not one of them." He paused, regarding the bewildered faces. He knew from his readings that these were a people who had lived with uncertainty and accepted it as immutable. Uncertainty, randomness, the inability to establish unbreakable guarantees despite modernity's progress—these were the reasons for today's pervading plague of "anxiety": that contemporary buzzword that had so dubiously been appropriated by profit-driven drug companies and their toady doctors. Once, Kevin had looked up "anxious" in a Victorian dictionary. In the mid-1890s it meant "being in painful suspense." For Kevin, this last term was prescient, as it seemed to sum up the television and Internet generations in four words. Didn't *everyone* these days go about their lives in a state of perpetual "painful suspense," spurred by the persistence of unmet desire and the more elusive and nagging need for pleasure that they continuously sought to satisfy? Wasn't the resultant tension and despair—the *anxiety*—a symptom of the idealized scenarios and empty promises manufactured and disseminated by advertisement-driven entertainment? And then there was the matter of speed. Everyone was speeding up. Speed itself had become a primary tenet of a supposedly successful modern life. There was the increased rate of speaking, the constant scrolling and swiping of screens, and along with this, the massive plummet in the percentage of the population that reads. A silent room with nothing but a shelf full of books had become a nightmare scenario for the majority of people of the early twenty-first century.

Kevin himself had instinctively rejected this unrestrained acceleration. The Heartstones had always owned a television and a phone and a computer, but these devices had never been the central features of the house. One of Kevin's earliest memories was of his father pointing to the television screen and saying, "That is human time, Kevin," and then to a window in the living room where a midsummer tree laden with waxy green leaves swayed a slow dance in the wind, "and that is *real* time." This central belief had left Kevin at odds with nearly every aspect of the modern world, which made concepts like trigger warnings, safe zones, binge watching, and not least, the proliferation of the Self via social media all the more bizarre. They were in many ways as alien to Kevin as they would be for these dead.

"And because of this, you see yourself as more enlightened than your contemporaries?" said Judge Cardinal.

"Not more enlightened, just living in reality. The real 'sickness' of my time is the inability of ordinary people to control their own addiction to pleasure. I've learned that the most important freedom—the only form of real control one has in a culture like this—is the freedom *not* to participate."

"Which is expressly why I invited him here, Father," Jane said turning to her father. "Kevin isn't like the others. He is sympathetic to our circumstances and wants to help us make contact."

"With whom, my dear? Those who are *not* 'sympathetic to our circumstances'?"

"We are *here,* are we not? Shall we remain in this decaying house, a place only slightly less dreary than our tombs, without even attempting to make contact to those outside it? Do we not have much to offer *them?*"

"We still do not know precisely *why* we've woken," the reverend added.

"The company that produces Plaiscene has been dumping by-product in semi-abandoned places like Treestone. Whatever is in it has caused a . . . reaction," Kevin said.

"An interesting theory, Mr. Heartstone. But it fails to account for our generally well-preserved states," said the judge.

"If my recollection is accurate, the site upon which Treestone now sits was utilized for the disposal of waste products as early as my first term in office," John Ellis Rodney said. "Perhaps, your honor, we hold as much responsibility for what has come to pass as the current generation."

"Perhaps, indeed," the judge said, his eyes drifting ponderously to the cracked plaster rose in the center of the ceiling.

"What if it has nothing to do with the boy's suppositions of a chemical interference? What if we are paradigms of the verity of holy divinity and the promise of everlasting life?" said the reverend.

"Are you suggesting this is Judgment Day, Reverend Vanquit?" Silas Leeds said.

"What if it is, Silas? Are you aware of any event more miraculous in the course of human history than that of us gathered in this room, decayed near to dust but with the capacity to think and reason? Can this be refuted as anything other than the work of the *Lord Himself?*"

"I for one hear no heralding bugles, nor see gilded chariots in the heavens to the east, Reverend," the judge said.

"It does not mean that God has abandoned us!" the reverend said fervently.

"Shall we proceed from this tedious subject? For how

many of us, including yourself, Reverend, passed the previous century and a half in a Christian kingdom of Heaven?" Silas bellowed.

A palpable silence fell over the room. Even Kevin thought about it, trying to imagine what it would be like to wake after a dreamless sleep of a hundred and fifty years, a vast bridge of Void connecting distant eras. While he was pondering this, he noticed a man standing in the shadows in the far right corner of the room. The man was staring at him. Kevin unzipped his backpack and took out the top hat. The crown was dented slightly from the trek through the city. He popped out the indentation and, as he was presenting it, realized suddenly where he'd seen the man's name before. He could picture it clearly, in high relief on a bronze plaque in a vast marble vestibule.

"You're William Mason Gladden, first librarian of the Still City Public Library."

William Gladden looked at Kevin, the stiff countenance unchanged. Then, slowly, his expression softened. It seemed to Kevin that Gladden was weeping, though no tears came. The dead man accepted the hat with a bow and put it on. The librarian held out his hand and Kevin shook it; it was cold, brittle, leathery—a thing generating no internal warmth. Particles of flaking skin like chipped paint remained on Kevin's hand after he let go. Kevin turned back to the faces in the room. He understood how he could help these people. What these dead truly wanted was not an explanation for why their buildings no longer stood, but why the *memory* of their own lives had been swept up along with the broken bricks and shards of ornamental bracket. They wished, merely, to know if anything of themselves had survived—not in history books or public records, but in living consciences. If they had made a difference for the future.

"I want to help," Kevin said. "I know the current mayor; he's a family friend. I can arrange a personal meeting with him and your representatives. He can offer protection

111

and will treat you with the same respect as any other citizen of this city. You will have a voice. You will have the opportunity to locate descendents, if you choose. It is up to you. If you decide to remain, you have my word that I will never reveal your whereabouts to anyone."

The judge regarded him silently for a long tense moment. Kevin glanced at Jane, saw her looking from him to her father, her thin pale fingers knotted just below her bodice. The stuffiness of the room was becoming stifling, as if the parlor itself was running out of air.

"We will convene on the matter," the judge said. "Look for our answer no later than evening tomorrow."

"I'll await your reply," Kevin said. He swallowed, then added. "Now . . . I shall go."

"You have always been free to leave, Mr. Heartstone," Silas Leeds said.

"I will see him out," Jane said, rising. She crossed the room, looping her arm through Kevin's, and guided him toward the hall. Kevin threw a last glance at the room crowded with the dead. All were looking at him, including the judge, his gaze unflinchingly sharp.

Kevin expected Jane to leave him off at the foyer, but she continued to walk with him out the front door and onto the porch. A brisk wind gusted in off the beach. The waning Cold Moon hung like a frozen pendulum, casting an iron gleam on the surface of the water. Kevin noticed there were also stars poking through the deepening dusk—a rare sight— though from this vantage point they shone plainly, unobstructed by the sallow city light and veils of green fog. He took in the entire panoramic sweep, from the lake-dominated north to the suburban south where the Interstate cut through gridded neighborhoods and then miles of dark, empty woods. At the center of this, in the east, stood the city, a glowing, seething cauldron.

"I want to come with you," Jane whispered.

Kevin turned to her. "Come with me?"

"Into the city. Into *your* world."

112

"How?"

Jane slid her arm down and threaded her cold fingers threading through his. "I thought you might assist me. Be my guide?"

"Your father would never allow it."

"My father will have no say," she said sharply. "We are all on our own now. We all must choose what we are to make of this time, however long or brief it might be. I will not waste it huddling in what is essentially another, larger tomb."

Kevin looked at the city. He could hear the hiss of traffic on the highway, the thrum of the steel plant, the stony roar of barges unloading along the riverbank. These were remote sounds; as one got closer a more intense cacophony became apparent: emergency sirens, droning generators, chirping phones, shouts and screams, and the insectile din of radios. Long gone were the clicking of carriage wheels, the cicadas and crickets in the surrounding pastures, the boson's whistle, the wind blowing through an empty town square at midnight. "I think you'll be disappointed by what you see."

"I am capable of making that judgment for myself," Jane said.

"Of course you are. I mean it's just that things are so dirty and ugly now . . ."

To this Jane said nothing. The obvious was easily discernible from her silence: she *wanted* to see it, whatever it was. She didn't care what he thought of it; she wanted to see it for herself. They stood silently side by side, Kevin trying desperately but failing to come up with a more pithy and substantive reason for his position. Finally Jane said: "It is unfair of me to ask this of you. I hope that you will forgive me for being so forward."

She turned back to the house, but Kevin refused to release her hand. They stood, hands joined, arms extended as if in a dance. Jane regarded him, her eyes firefly bright. Kevin felt himself trembling again, thinking: *please don't let go*. It was desperate, this plea, threaded to some vulnerable place inside him he hadn't known was there. He drew her toward him, relieved that she let herself be drawn. They looked at each other in the fading crepuscule, two natives of the city of the same age separated by over a century and a half, each considering that mystery. One thing was certain: she could not pass through the city without being noticed. She would have to be, as much as it pained him to think it, *modernized.*

"All right," he said. "I'll show you. But I think we'll need some help."

Jane smiled. There was *life* in that smile, a resurrection of hope. She glanced back at the house. "We must hurry. They'll be curious as to why I have not returned and will soon come looking."

Kevin removed his coat, pulled his father's hooded sweatshirt over his head, and put it on Jane. The sleeves were too long, and the elastic bottom band reached almost to her knees, covering her upper half and most of her old-fashioned dress. The sweatshirt didn't conceal the waxy yellow/gray flesh of her legs or her leather boots with their recurved heels. But it would be full dark soon, and there were far stranger creatures prowling the roads and avenues of Still City.

He took her hand again and together they hurried down the stairs and across the dead lawn toward the gate. Jane's hand was cold in his, though it grew warmer, taking on his warmth, the longer he held it.

4

The van was parked in the furthest space from the lane, headlights off, backed in so that the woods obscured the rear and passenger sides. The two men sat in bucket seats watching through night-vision goggles for the kid to emerge. They didn't know why they were being told to wait, now that they'd finally located the contagion. The captain had known that it was no longer in the cemetery, knew that the guards posted at its gates were a ruse, for despite the round-the-clock security, no one else came and went. No researchers, no archaeologists, no doctors—no one. He'd had a feeling about the boy on the news and had immediately sent the men after him, Nazgûl-like. The captain had been right: the boy had led them right to the source. They'd tracked him through the woods, saw him enter the house with that . . . figure.

That had been almost an hour ago. The men were hungry, groggy, each still dealing with the remnants of a hangover even though it was well into evening. It had been two weeks since either of them had had a proper night's sleep. They hadn't been hired for this. They were *security guards*. But the promise of promotion, not to mention being in good standing with the captain, had been intoxicating inducements. Yet increasingly they'd been complaining to each other, declaring that the promised advancements had better be worth all the bullshit . . .

They were thick into one of these bitch sessions when the boy, accompanied by a girl in a long sweatshirt with the hood pulled up, appeared at the end of the lane. They crossed the length of the parking lot quickly, passing right in front of the van. One of the men picked up his phone, pressed a button. The captain answered after a single ring.

"The mice are leaving the forest," the man said.

"Mice?"

"Yes. The boy, and one of . . . *them*."

A long pause on the other end. Then: "Let them scurry. We will find them later. Destroy the nest. Make sure the others do not scatter," the captain said, followed by a click—then silence. The man holding the phone put it down, then nodded once to the other man. They got out and went around to the unobstructed side and opened the panel door. Inside stood four large red plastic containers. They each grabbed two and started off toward the lane. The containers were heavy; the men walked hunched like gorillas through the brambles. When they reached the end they split off, each taking one side of the house, splashing accelerant along their respective perimeters, and then meeting up again at the porch, where they tossed the containers along with a lit pack of matches. The blast of the igniting fumes singed the hair on their faces. In less than a minute the flames had risen up the sides of the house like scaffolding.

The two men stood at a distance, guns drawn, watching the place burn. They'd been told to remain, to make sure no one escaped. But the prospect of *them* coming out, flaming or otherwise, was in the end too ghastly to consider, and after only a few seconds they fled back to the van. As they sped away, the conflagrant house seemed to swell in the rearview mirror, a great funeral pyre blazing against the black sky of a dying year.

5

Coletta Hughes lay on her bed, battered novel in hand, staring at page 98, which she'd read absently three times. Everything seemed to distract her: the garish overhead light of her faux wood-paneled bedroom; the muted voices and canned laughter of the television in the next room; the greasy fishy stink permeating the apartment. Demetrius, her mother's boyfriend, had brought a dripping plastic sack of walleye along with his nightly six-pack of Old Steed tall boys and had spent the afternoon gutting both the fish and the beers.

She got up and opened the room's only window, which led to the building's fire escape and overlooked an empty unkempt lot flanked by an abandoned insurance agency and a recently burned beauty salon. She could still smell the charred wood on the cold wind as it wafted into the apartment, mixing with the reek of fried fish. Outside sounds joined the drone of the television, but they were white noise to her: the buzz of the power lines, the hiss of traffic, the low moaning wind counterpointed by warbling sirens shrieking at varying distances. There were always sirens.

She plopped back down on the bed and sat propped up against some pillows. The room had cooled off, the smell dispersed somewhat. She picked up the book and began to

116

read, though soon her mind began to drift again. This time it was thoughts of that boy which distracted her. Part of her wished she'd gone with him. Except on TV, she hadn't seen any of the dead people supposedly roaming the city. They hadn't looked real to her; she thought it was probably a media stunt. The reason she'd gone to Treestone earlier that day was to check on the plots of her ancestors—to make sure they weren't being toppled and trampled upon in all this craziness. Her passion for their memory had stemmed from an interest in her own origins, a need to piece together a narrative from the shards of her fractured family history. Her mother, Rondella Hughes, descended from slaves. For over a year Coletta had assumed the onerous task of researching her maternal side—the Hughes side—only to hit the dreaded "wall of 1870": the first year the national census counted freed blacks and listed them by name. Any count of enslaved peoples before that year had included only descriptions and numbers; they hadn't been considered individuals after all, but *commodities*.

Her father's side had been much easier to track. Her fourth great-grandfather, John Ellis Rodney, was born free in 1842, the son of a black freedwoman and her white former master. John had grown up in the North, attended university, and had gone on to become one of the first black senators in the country's history. His son had become a politician as well, and Coletta's great-grandfather and grandfather had been prominent Still City attorneys. Her own father, Ernest Rodney Jr., had been the first eldest son in three generations to eschew college, attending a trade school against his father's wishes, where he studied to become a welder. Ernest Sr. had consequently severed relations with his son and in the end left him out of his will.

Rondella and Ernest Jr. dated for less than a year, during which their only child was conceived. They never married. Ernest Jr. was electrocuted while his crew was repairing a bridge when Coletta was four. Her only memories of her father were the low, rhythmic hum of his voice and the way his work shirt stank of electrode slag. Because of his blue-collar career choice, he was buried not in the family plot, but in a west side cemetery established for the poor, which took three different buses and a half-hour walk to reach from the east side. Coletta had only been to her father's grave twice in her life: once the year after he died, and again on some random fall afternoon that she later learned was some sort of anniversary, though that was as forthcoming as her mother was on the subject. The bronze plaque (the only funerary contribution from Ernest Jr.'s estranged father) was almost hidden by October leaves, which mother and daughter swept away, noticing that the monument had settled crooked and was already beginning to oxidize. Coletta, seven at the time, stared at the sober capitals of her father's name, those letters so final, immutable. To read them was to feel them branded into her heart. She could still recall her mother's expression, which at the time had seemed distant, even indifferent. But to reflect on it now was to observe a peculiar complexity that her child's mind hadn't the ability to discern. What had once appeared apathetic she recognized now to be masterful restraint—the face of a woman stripped of illusions and dreams, of her faith even; the shrewd, vulture-eyed stare of one whose grief had set hard as the concrete foundation housing Ernest Jr.'s burial plate. It seemed to Coletta authentic bravery—and she'd tried to mimic it from that day on.

Coletta's life after her father's death had been like those of many others in her neighborhood: one of privation and abject hopelessness. Her mother worked a handful of low-paying jobs over the years to support them, two or three at a time—passing through the metal detectors at the nearby high school to scoop utility-grade meat onto cafeteria trays by day, and by night, cashiering at the Dollar Saver. On the weekends, she was a housekeeper at an hourly-rate motel. Coletta saw her mother during the two hours between shifts and in the late evening when they watched television together before bed: Rondella collapsed in her tan recliner, catatonic-

118

eyed, her feet swollen, the bottoms of her ashy heels cracked. Often she'd fall asleep in the chair, where she'd remain until Coletta woke her at 7 A.M.

Thus, Coletta's was a childhood à la the old days, accustomed to Duty rather than whimsical daydreaming. The world became Real for her before she understood it to be any other way. At the age of six she had her own house key, was packing her own lunch, and picking her outfits for school. By nine she was stopping at the corner store that stank of stale beer and pot to pick up the grocery items her mother had scrawled on a list and left on the faded laminate countertop along with a few gritty bills. She made dinner and did the dishes, vacuumed, swept, scrubbed the bathroom. She did her homework by herself, at the second-hand kitchen table with a glass of powdered mix lemonade and the radio on so that the apartment wasn't so spookily silent. She carried the dirty clothes down four floors to the scary, musty basement where the washer and dryer were and heaved them all in together: her dollar-store tops and kid's pants tumbling with her mother's red work smocks and food-stained school uniforms and fraying blue jeans that stank of motel disinfectant and second-hand smoke. Shy and friendless in school and isolated in the quotidian gloom of home, Coletta went in search of kinship, some semblance of connection to family, living or dead, which she found in nearby Treestone Cemetery.

She located the neglected Rodney plot at the center of Treestone's northwest quadrant under the cloak-like boughs of a massive spruce. The section, hemmed by a low cast iron fence, was so overgrown that only the tops of the grave markers were visible. Atop one had been a line of snuffed-out cigarette butts. At the center of the family plot was a black granite obelisk standing on a plinth of the same material and surrounded by several small stones whose rounded white tops jutted out of the ground like milk teeth. On the tops of these, in low relief, was "mother" and "father" and "son" and "daughter," etc. These were Coletta's uncles and aunts and cousins and grandmothers and grandfathers. Despite its

119

derelict state, Coletta felt a bloom of love unfurl within her. This was *her* family, *her* blood. While researching them, she discovered that they had been formidable figures, foundations of the modern city, trailblazers, equal rights pioneers, liberty seekers. Their lives had been crucibles of unimaginable adversity and illimitable courage.

Over the years, caring for the plot had become more than a remedy for loneliness, more than merely the sum of clipping and washing and arranging tributes. Coletta learned what it meant to be a steward of memory. It was a personal undertaking, a solemn passion whose true rewards were intangible and immaterial. It was a task that, she believed, confirmed the existence of the soul and promulgated its relevance through the ages. It was a confirmation of love. So she tended their graves, scrubbing the stones and trimming the grass, pulling weeds and even (in later years) repainting the ornate perimeter fence. She planted fresh flowers in the summer and laid holly berry and evergreen wreaths in the winter.

When she'd seen the previous night's news report, saw the chains and the temporary barriers and the posted warnings, she'd decided to go the following day to make sure that the plot had not been disturbed. And when she'd found it barricaded and arm-guarded—when she'd read the seriousness of the situation in those men's eyes—hadn't her heart quickened with half dread/half thrill? Hadn't she, from that moment, *believed?* This had made the denial of access all the more frustrating. To think that they were actually *in there* walking around, or, as Coletta for some reason had pictured them (the shriveled skin, the rotted clothing, the green eyes regarding her warmly as she approached), having tea and sandwiches picnic-style on the snow amongst Christmas wreaths she'd placed a week earlier. It was silly, the sandwiches and all—but she liked the image, and entertained it nonetheless.

Now she thought of the boy, Kevin Heartstone, who claimed to have received a letter and was going to meet one of them and he'd invited Coletta and she had just walked away from him. Why had she done that? Sitting on her bed, the novel in her lap now closed, she laughed to herself thinking how fitting that it was *that* boy who was somehow the link to all this. He was the only one in her school who seemed to give a damn about something other than cell phones and social media. For months she'd sat staring at the back of his head in seventh-period Historical Foundations, sending out mental signals like some crazed mesmerist in an attempt to get him to turn around. She flashed on being alone with him in that wrecked house earlier in the day, of the sheen of sweat on his skin, of the deep hard breaths they drew together, exhausted from running. Though cold air continued to gust through the window, Coletta felt suddenly flushed.

There was a knock on her door—it was Demetrius. He stood in the doorway dressed in the outfit he wore invariably: a white A-shirt and black sweatpants. He'd brought some food for her—a plate with enough fried walleye on it to feed a family of five. *No thanks,* she said, *I'm not hungry.* Demetrius shrugged the way he usually did—a shrug that seemed to say "I just don't get this girl"—and closed the door behind him.

Coletta got up, went to the window, and looked out onto the cratered band of blacktop that was Eloise Street. It was four days from Christmas, but up and down the road there were no decorations on the rundown houses, no Happy Holidays banners on the city telephone poles, no red and green lights except for the traffic signal strung from a piece of fraying wire across the nearest intersection. She regarded this as if from the porthole of a ship set adrift, without power, without hope of rescue. For the first time in her life, she realized that *this* might be all there was, that despite her attempts to free herself from the cyclic pattern of discrimination and poverty by getting good grades and staying clear of the manifold dangers ubiquitous in an impoverished city district, she would ultimately end up like her mother: a single parent, a braveheart struggling through a string of low-income jobs. A martyr of the ghetto.

The phone rang in the kitchen. Coletta heard her mother answer it after ten rings. There was a pause, then footsteps coming towards the bedroom door.

"You awake?" Rondella said.

"Yeah."

"Someone on the phone for you."

"For *me?*"

"Some girl."

Coletta's heart sank. For just an instant, she had been hoping—

"Coming," she said.

The phone was mounted on a column between the kitchen and living room. The receiver lay button-side-up on the counter that jutted out from the column. Coletta slid around it to the kitchen side, wedged herself in the corner between the wall and the yolk yellow Formica, and picked up the receiver.

"Hello?"

"Hey, it's me."

She frowned. The voice was *male*. She didn't recognize it, not at first.

"Who?"

"It's *Kevin.*"

"How did you get my number?"

"From the phone book. Listen, I need your help."

"With what?"

"With . . ." Kevin hesitated. "It has to do with what we talked about earlier."

"Where are you?"

"At a phone booth right now, but about to head to the library."

"I'm not sure that I can sneak out . . ."

"*Please.* We need you."

We. The word was simultaneously terrifying and thrilling. Coletta glanced over her shoulder at her mother and

Demetrius, each in a pair of battered reclining chairs positioned in front of the television, each with a plate of fried fish and coleslaw in their lap. The side table between them was cluttered with condiments and remote controls and a tabletop Christmas tree strung with mini Old Steed beer can lights that Demetrius had won it in a convenience store giveaway. A real beer, frosted with condensation, stood beside Rondella Hughes's sixty-four-ounce plastic mug filled with cubed ice and diet soda. By all appearances, they were settled in for the night.

"There might be a way."

"Can you make it before eight?"

"I'll do my best."

"Excellent. We'll be upstairs. Bring some of your clothes. And . . . some makeup."

The line clicked off. *Makeup?* Coletta softly hung up the phone, walked around the counter, and stood where linoleum met carpet—the demarcation line of kitchen and living room in the little apartment.

"Ma, I'm not feeling good. I'm gonna go to bed."

Rondella looked up from her plate. "What's wrong, baby?"

"Nothing serious, just—" Coletta broke off, hovered her hands over her lower abdominal region. Her mother glanced there, hesitated, then nodded.

"See you in the morning," Coletta said.

"Who was that on the phone?" her mother called after her.

"A girl from class."

Rondella took a bite of fish and chewed slowly. Coletta saw the lie caught in her mother's eyes like a fly in a web. Girls from class never called the house. Suddenly her mother winced, groaned, then opened her mouth and pulled out a thin but sizable bone. "*Damn,* Deemee, thought you said you cleaned these!" She tossed her plate on the side table next to the mini tree and threw the bone at Demetrius, who chuckled.

123

Coletta used the distraction to slip out of the room back to her own. She grabbed an old backpack from her closet and began stuffing random clothing into it: T-shirts, sweatshirts, a skirt, leggings, sneakers. Lastly she added her cosmetic pouch, then zipped up the bag, put on a pair of shoes and her heavy coat. Before leaving the room she flipped the radio on and stuffed some pillows under the bed covers in a vaguely human shape. It felt silly doing this, clichéd, not likely to work, but she reasoned that it was better than not doing it. Then she opened the window and stepped cautiously out onto the fire escape. It was rickety and unstable and clattered like a stack of wire hangers as she crept down the grated stairs, which terminated at the bottom of the building's second level. There was a ladder but it was frozen to the landing, so Coletta took a deep breath, slid her legs over the edge, gripped the metal slats, and extended herself as far as she could before letting go.

She landed hard, but the bag cushioned the impact. She got to her feet, took a few steps back, and looked up at her bedroom window, half expecting to see her mother's head poking out. Busted. But her room was dark, and the window closed, along with the rest in the building. Everyone was shut in on this cold Solstice night.

There was a drone in the dark—Coletta saw the approaching bus lights and ran the twenty or so yards to the nearest stop, reaching the downtown bound number 57 just in time.

6

There was a narrow passage on the second floor of the Still City Public Library between the reference room and the last shelf of the fiction section where a reading area had been set up—a half dozen round tables, each with four chairs. No one really used it. Though one of the compass windows along the building's rear wall was centered in the passage, it was partly obscured by a neighboring building, and the light was poor.

At sundown it became downright gloomy, and the industrial overhead fluorescents did little to diffuse the shadows that gathered in the space like smoke.

It was Kevin's favorite part of the library, the place where he could spread out an armful of books and delve into his studies. He felt invisible there, particularly at the back of the passage where he had watched people walk by without a glance, as if they didn't even notice the area was there. And it was where Kevin now sat with Jane, who still wore his sweatshirt though with the hood pulled down. Kevin was starving. He hadn't eaten since breakfast and now all he could think of was the granola bar crushed under the books at the bottom of his bag.

"Would you mind if I eat something?"

"You do not require my permission," Jane said.

"I know. It just seems rude . . ."

She flashed a faint smile. "Never let manners supersede necessity, Mr. Heartstone."

"That doesn't sound in keeping with your time."

"Nevertheless, it's what I have always believed."

Kevin nodded, reached in his bag, and grabbed the granola bar. The wrapper made a clatter like heavy rain in the total silence. He quietly folded it after he ate and stuffed it in his coat pocket, then checked his pocket watch. It had been forty five minutes since he'd called Coletta, and the library closed in less than an hour. What would he do if she didn't come? He could feel Jane's eyes on him, studying him. She seemed fascinated by even his smallest movement. A part of Kevin liked the attention, though it also made him exceedingly self-conscious. He found himself picking at his fingernails and constantly glancing at the beginning of the passage for Coletta.

"You're rather nervous," Jane observed.

"I am, a little," he confessed.

"It is my fault. It was selfish of me to ask this of you."

"No, it's not because of you," Kevin said. "I guess I'm feeling a little guilty because my mother doesn't know where I am and I've been gone all day . . ."

"Tell me about her. What is her name?" Jane said.

"Jenna. She's an industrial pharmacist."

"I am not familiar with that occupation."

"She develops new drugs, including the one that's responsible for you being here."

"It sounds as though she is a woman of great importance."

Kevin shrugged. "I guess." He paused, then said: "What about your mother? Did she . . . come back too?"

Jane glanced somberly at the darkened window, her luminescent eyes remaining there as she spoke. "When I Woke, the first thing I beheld was my father gazing down at me. I was not sure what had taken place, for he had watched over me in the same manner night after night during my illness, and initially it seemed as though I were still in my bed, convalescing. Rather quickly, however, I began to comprehend that something singular had occurred. My father's appearance was out of character. He was disheveled, his face oddly withered, and his eyes shone green, though they had always been chestnut in color. I looked down at my hands, which were folded and grasping brittle, colorless blooms. My bed was no longer curtained, but sided with low walls trimmed in shriveled lace. Suddenly I was overwhelmed with panic. I sat up, opening my mouth as if to gasp though no air penetrated my lungs. They had become stone doors; yet soon it became apparent that I need draw no breath. Indeed, I placed a palm to my chest, which was still and eburnated. It was a grievous fright. My father continued to stand beside me, calmly, as one by one I grasped these epiphanies. I remember asking: 'Where are we, Father?'

"'Rise, my child,' he replied, 'rise and be reborn.'"

Approaching footsteps sounded in the corridor beyond the passage. Kevin and Jane looked up as a man shuffling papers walked by without a glance in their direction.

"The door to the mausoleum was open," Jane continued, "emitting a gray light by which I saw the three iron coffins, including my own, set atop stone daises. My father assisted me out."

"How did you feel? I mean, was it painful?" Kevin asked.

"I was able to hear, and see him rather clearly, but it was beyond my capacity to *feel* him. Only the slightest tingling sensation could be attained, and that when great pressure was applied. Together, we went to my mother's coffin. Great was my anticipation as I watched my father work the latch. Oh, to see her again, my sweet dear mother! Taken from us so suddenly as she had been, without the opportunity for departing words. When he opened it, however, his expression was not that of joy but horror. He staggered back, almost falling; but I caught him, and in the same moment surmised the strength in my frame, for though my limbs were leaden and without feeling, they contained an immense power: they felt solid like the branches of a great oak. I steadied him, leaned him against one of the stone slabs, then I moved toward the coffin.

"He cried: 'Do not look, Jane!' His exclamation of grief was an attempt to spare me the sight of what lay within: not the beloved visage of my mother, but a shallow pool of inky sludge."

Picking at the cuticle of his right thumb, Kevin drew blood and brought it to his lips. He'd read about the kind of caskets Jane described, ones that claimed to arrest decay and perfectly preserve the body. Though in some cases this had actually worked, overwhelmingly the design had failed, resulting not in a Sleeping Beauty corpse, but one transformed into bones or adipocere or, like Jane's mother, "coffin liquor." Some of these devices promising corporeal immortality had even exploded, their lids blown off by the pressure of built-up post-mortem gases. The articles, tracts, columns, studies, had described these phenomena, medicalized them, though hardly considered them in personal or emotional terms. For Kevin there was a deep, seam-tearing sensation internally when considering the fate of physical remains. Often he'd wondered what his father must look like, now four years underground. When he was younger he pictured a perfect skeleton dressed in that awkward suit like some elaborate department store Halloween prop. But the more he read, the more he came to comprehend the ghoulish reality of what occurred after burial, and why indeed it was relegated to six feet under. Still, on the few occasions he'd come across the photo of an exhumed body, Kevin had found himself absurdly searching for something supra-mortal in the long-entombed cadaver, as if it had attained some arcane enlightenment while underground—answers, perhaps, to what lay beyond the dismal actuality of decomposition.

He looked at Jane, half illumined by a hard slant of street light passing through the compass window. It had begun to snow again. Along with the flake shadows flitting across her sunken visage Kevin saw pain. He also saw what he'd been searching for, what had been missing from those ghastly exhumation pictures: life. It was so simple, so obvious it made him feel ridiculous. The dead no longer suffered, though they continued to *cause* suffering. He was alive and Jane (in one way or another) was alive and that was why they suffered.

"I'm sorry that you had to experience that," Kevin said.

Jane smiled. It was brief, but endearing. Even in death she was beautiful. He reckoned that, had she lived, she would have been a stunning woman.

"You are gracious. Perhaps it was foolish to entertain such high expectations. But it saddened me to behold her so reduced. I was grateful for having been fortunate in retaining my father. I went to him, took his hand, and led him to my mother's coffin. There, we said a short prayer, one more personal than holy in nature, in which we professed our love for her and confirmed our eternal remembrance before together closing the lid."

"It sounds nice. I wish I had had that chance. I mean, a private opportunity," Kevin said.

"Your father . . ." Jane said.

Kevin frowned. "You know about him?"

Jane looked guiltily into her lap. "From your writings."

Of course—she had read his commonplace book. That self-conscious feeling returned; he started picking at the cuticle where a fresh bead of blood had just begun to coagulate.

"I do hope that you will forgive me," Jane said, then added: "You have a lovely penmanship."

"Actually, I am glad that you read it. I've felt increasingly isolated over the last few years. As if no one *knows* me. It's not like I don't want to talk to people. They just seem so lost in their own thing all the time. And they definitely don't want to talk about sad things, like dead fathers. Sometimes it gets so bad it's like . . . I feel like I'm already dead."

"I have myself despaired in a similar manner, during my former life as well as the span between it and this one—"

"You mean you . . . *were somewhere?*" Kevin said.

"Yes."

"But what about the others? Why didn't they claim to know anything when Mayor Leeds asked them?"

"If you recall, he asked them if they had any memory of a Christian kingdom of heaven."

Kevin thought a moment, then nodded. "Where were you, Jane?"

"There was darkness, though not . . . stillness. It was textured, velvety, similar to a very rich, very black soil, though that comparison still fails to describe it accurately. Across this tenebrous firmament an industrious constellation of magnificent colors, rainbow-bright, unfurled and intertwined. They grew and receded, transformed and diffused at differing rates, in shades and shapes—some of which I had never beheld in life. I likened them to seedlings blossoming into diverse patterns of inflorescence, all communicating, all from the same source, though that source was hidden from me.

For a long time I was not certain what I was witnessing. Was this an esoteric drawing of worlds, a mapping of life cycles, a sketching of galaxies? Or was it something much smaller, perhaps microscopic? And was it past or was it future? I pondered this while hanging in balance, on reserve or so it felt, watching these configurations blazing the courses of their prescribed eons, until one of the colors burned most brilliant of all, and I was pulled toward it."

"And then?" Kevin said. He was shaking.

"Then I was here."

"Looking at your father."

Jane nodded.

"When did you discover that there were others?"

"We were among the first to Wake. It was dawn; my father led me to the door of our little crypt and I peered out into the cemetery, morosely surveying the crumbling tombs and decayed grave markers, and then I looked beyond, at the strange austere houses and steel vehicles and the towers like fairytale castles high as the spire of Babel."

Kevin leaned toward her. "What did you think when you saw them? When you understood what had happened?"

"I thought it was wondrous," Jane said.

The man shuffling papers walked past again. This time he stopped, paused, stared in their direction for several moments. "The library closes in thirty minutes," he said.

"Oh. Thank you," Kevin said. In his periphery he saw the man hesitate, observing them from his distance. *What if he saw her eyes?* Kevin thought. His heart began to race. He looked up, expecting to see the man coming closer but he had already moved on.

"We should go," Kevin whispered.

"But your friend—how will she find us?"

"I don't think she's coming. Maybe you should pull your hood up again. Just to be safe."

Jane looked at Kevin for a long moment, then composed herself, folded her hands primly in her lap, and said: "No. I don't think so."

130

"But what if he comes back? What if they *see* you?"

"Then they shall see me! I no longer wish to hide. I am ready to face this age, come what may."

The sound of footsteps returned in the corridor. They were measured, seeking. In Kevin's mind he saw the librarian returning with a security guard, flashlight raised, gun drawn. They would take Jane away.

"*Please,* Jane!" Kevin hissed.

But Jane did not move. She sat in a fixed posture, head cocked slightly toward the end of the passage, awaiting with equanimity whatever came around the corner. Despite his panic, Kevin admired her poise and resolve. He himself, however, could not look as the figure approached; only when it was near their table did Kevin see that it was not in fact a guard, but Coletta. She wore a black wool coat zipped to her chin and her hair pulled back in a tight ponytail. Her face was long and angular, fine-lined and solemn as an Egyptian bust. She smelled of bus fumes and something faintly floral; it was an old-fashioned scent, like eau-de-rose. Her eyes and nose were watery from the cold. Kevin stood, his first instinct was to embrace her—strangely, she already felt like a friend—though in the end he held back.

"We don't have much time. Did you bring clothes and makeup?" he asked.

Coletta didn't answer. She was staring at Jane.

"Did you bring clothes and makeup?" Kevin repeated. Now Coletta looked at him, her eyes drifting in his direction as if she'd been woken from a trance. She held up the backpack.

"Good," Kevin said. He moved between them so that his back was to Jane. "We need to make her look like she belongs . . . you know . . . 'today.' Do you think you can do that?" he said softly.

"I'll try," Coletta said. Kevin saw her hands trembling.

"There's a bathroom around the corner," Kevin said. He turned around and looked at Jane. "Are you ready?"

"Yes," she said, rising. Kevin watched them walk side

by side down the passage and disappear around the corner.

He sat down again but only for a minute or so—his stomach felt too nervous. He got up and began wandering down the aisles, browsing the stacks without paying much attention to the titles. At some point, as he reached a shelf end cap, he saw Coletta and Jane. The same man who had given Kevin and Jane the thirty-minute warning passed the girls as they emerged from the restroom. He informed them also that the library was closing, without a second look at Jane. It was plain why. The girl who now walked beside Coletta appeared as unassuming as any tenth grader at Clinton High: white sweater, black jeans, low-cut tennis shoes, a blue coat with the collar raised, and her long hair brushed out and spilling over her shoulders. Coletta had applied a heavy golden matte foundation, a touch of color to Jane's lips (subtle, not enough to draw attention), and a pair of lightly shaded sunglasses that dimmed Jane's luminescent eyes. Lastly, Kevin noticed Jane was still wearing the coral necklace. It actually complemented the rest of the ensemble.

"He did not notice me!" Jane said excitedly. "How do you find it, Kevin? Do I appear quite . . . *modern?*"

"Yes. It's *amazing*," Kevin said. He looked at Coletta. "Really, really amazing."

"It wasn't that difficult," Coletta conceded.

They walked downstairs, passing the reference desk in the main lobby. The woman working it did not look up. Jane regarded her disappointedly, then suddenly broke away from them and approached the desk.

"What time's the library open tomorrow?" she asked. Kevin noticed her modified syntax and the attempt at a contemporary accent. She was learning fast.

The woman looked up; her eyes fixed on Jane and there was a moment of pause, but Kevin saw no suspicion in them. "Nine A.M.," the woman said tiredly and went back to sorting her books.

"Thank you," Jane said, grinning. "Thank you very much indeed."

The three left the library together, exiting into the brisk December night, and stood at the top of the granite stair facing Central Square. It was the last weekend for shopping before the holiday, and the place was mobbed. Traffic moaned at a crawl through the clogged streets, interspersed by throngs of shoppers with armfuls of bags and boxes. Skaters moved at varying speeds along the surface of the ice rink that lay like a frosted eyeglass lens beneath the towering statue of Wilhelm DeStill, his tri-cornered hat crowned with a laurel of snow. Many of the surrounding skyscrapers had left their lights on; other lights—crystal bulbs and warm saturated color bulbs and the cold, crisp hues of LEDs—festooned the square in brilliant garlands. The air was heavy with car and restaurant exhaust, the sound of sung carols, and the relentless yet pleasantly festive jingle of the charity bucket ringers.

"Well, where do you want to go?" Kevin asked.

"Everywhere," Jane said.

*

They had little money; not enough to do anything really except wander amongst the crowds, window-gazing and people-watching. Kevin and Coletta found this tedious and even a tad irritating, but for Jane there wasn't a single detail that wasn't wholly engrossing. The world had become a colossus, an unprecedented display of engineering and technological marvels that to Jane rivaled, and in many cases surpassed, the Ancients. Marble columns were replaced by girders and pylons of reinforced steel, combining to create structures vertiginous in scale. Hundreds of pod-like machines, streamlined and sleek like poured liquid color, raced from one end of town to the other and beyond. Plane contrails streaked the sky. Everything was powered and lit by the harnessed, ceaseless flow of electrical current. The people of this age strode about their creations with a mix of haughtiness and self-congratulation archetypal of a formidable society.

Jane noticed these things, while at the same time noticing what was no longer there. The blocks of Italianate brick and stone buildings with their quaint signage; the quiet dirt streets; the church spires; the green areas. There was no smell of soot, no gaslights, no dirt roads littered with horse dung, though she was shocked to find a single horse-drawn carriage operating amongst the cars and motorbikes. Two haggard white mares, heads bowed in shackled subservience and sheer exhaustion, stood in the falling snow at the head of a cabriolet driven by a corpulent man dressed in an ill-fitting and anachronistic suit—the entire scene a shoddy parody of times past. Jane pitied the poor animals. They were personifications of broken will, trudging alongside the groaning engines, hardly spurred by the nagging crack of the fat man's whip. When she asked Kevin *Why?* he told her people rode in those carriages to feel "nostalgic"—a notion that only puzzled her further.

Coletta was fascinated watching Jane. Despite the modern clothing, Jane's corset posture made her stand out. She walked with her hands clasped at her navel, elbows akimbo, strolling slowly as if hindered by skirts. They entered a café; Coletta and Jane found a booth at the far end of the room, and Kevin ordered three hot chocolates at the counter. He brought them back and slid into the seat across from the girls, doling out the steaming mugs. Kevin and Coletta sipped the cocoa. Jane held her mug, warming her hands with it, but did not drink from.

"Where is that music coming from?" Jane asked.

"See those black boxes mounted in the corners behind the bar?" Kevin said. Jane located them, nodded. "They're called speakers. They're part of a sound system that amplifies and projects music and voices."

Coletta added: "From either a recording or a live broadcast. Sounds are captured onto a device and then played back. Or they're transmitted digitally or over radio waves."

"Are these systems similar to the telegraph?" Jane said.

"In concept, though a thousand times more complex," Kevin said.

"And those small square machines everyone carries? Are those 'speakers' as well?"

"That's one element, perhaps the most basic . . ."

Kevin had finished most of his hot chocolate by the time he'd explained the general evolution of twentieth-century communicative technology. Coletta chimed in occasionally about television and film. On Jane's request, they both described an average day in their respective lives in full detail, including school, meals, the bus, family, and life in the city.

"We're considered poor, but we have everything we need," Coletta said with regard to herself and her mother.

"And your father?" Jane said.

"Died when I was a girl," Coletta said.

"What about you, Kevin? Have you been as fortunate as she?"

Kevin shrugged. "I suppose." Coletta flashed him a look that he thought might have been a scowl.

"What year were you born, Jane?" Coletta said.

"1845."

"And when—" Kevin started, though he did not finish. It seemed rude to ask what that second number was— the one on the right of the hyphen on her headstone. It also seemed a strange question, seeing as that she was sitting across from him.

"I believe, Mr. Heartstone, you were about to inquire as to the date of my death. It is all right to ask. 1860."

"Before the war," Coletta said, turning to Kevin.

"War?" Jane said.

"It started when a group of southern states seceded and became the Confederacy. The fighting went on for four years and resulted in over a million casualties and six hundred thousand deaths. In 1863 President Lincoln abolished slavery and two years later the Union Army defeated the Confederacy," Kevin said.

"The slaves were free then, after this war?" Jane asked.

"They were free, but hardly considered equal," Coletta said.

Kevin looked at her. "I met your grandfather."

Coletta gazed back at him, eyes misting. "What is he like?"

"He's everything you've read, and more."

"I want to meet him," Coletta said, looking at Jane.

"I will see what can be arranged," Jane said.

The bell over the café door jingled. Kevin looked up as two men dressed in identical plain black clothes came in. One was scruffy and blond, the other had a laser line skull cap of black hair. They walked toward the counter, the blond guy staring at Kevin and the girls as they settled onto a pair of stools across from the table. They ordered coffees from the barista and sipped them in silence. Kevin looked at the sludgy chocolate dregs in his cup, feeling increasingly anxious though he wasn't sure why. He tried to focus on what Coletta and Jane were now discussing, something about Jane's memory of what the city used to look like.

"We lived in a large, fine house built by my grandfather. He was a member of the DeStill party which initially scouted this region. I noticed we are currently on East Eleventh and Progress. If the city plan is the same, the house once stood just a block from this very spot. I began attending Johnson's Seminary, three miles distant, at the age of thirteen. It was there that I contracted typhus. The town itself was in those years rather modest in scale. Humble, yet prosperous. I believe the census at the time counted fewer than forty thousand souls. The business district was a collection of storefronts surrounded by small parks with crisscrossing walkways and churches. The steeples of the latter were the highest peaks, affirming their rank. There were rows of young oaks and sycamores and hickories and one marvelous weeping willow that grew before the fountain in the original town square. I can recall the smell of the lake blowing in through the muddy streets. The ports burgeoned; the sound of ships arriving and departing was perpetual. On the whole, it was a proper and respectable town, steadily growing in refinement."

"Yes, it *was*," Kevin sighed.

Jane regarded him curiously. "And is it not still?"

"You know the answer to that. You've seen it for yourself," Kevin said.

"I have indeed. What I've witnessed is astounding."

"Astounding? You're referring to the level of decay and destruction and general state of degradation, I assume?"

"Quite the contrary. True, those aspects are regrettable, but there must be absolution for sacrificing the past if posterity necessitates it."

"It's this presumed *necessity* that I have the biggest problem with," Kevin said. "The city you once knew has all but been erased except for a building or two. In most cases there have been several different buildings erected on the same site, built and torn down again and again. For what? There was *value* in what your people made. No one respects that today."

"And is there no value in *now*, Kevin? What of the qualities of your own age? Too much time and effort spent revering *what was* is not advisable, my friend. The past is a lonely place, populated by ghosts. I beg you, heed this warning, or you will live a detached life, devoid of community save for your own bitter prejudgments."

"I revere those ghosts because they appreciated quality, style, and durability. Did you know that the oldest house in this city is currently condemned and filled with garbage? Vinyl sided, with a broken satellite dish bolted to the roof. That's not what I call *necessity*."

"No, that is merely that house's fate. We all must come to pass, Kevin. People and objects alike."

"Should we just cast you and the others aside then? Regard you as mere relics dressed in moldy suits, without merit or import?"

"Kevin," Coletta hissed.

"How like us you speak," Jane said darkly. "I wonder how many precious hours of your youth you have squandered imitating phantoms."

"I have never considered a moment of my studies to be time wasted. It's the reason I feel close to your century. It's why I'm sympathetic to what's happening to you and the others and why I want to help."

"If you know us, then you are aware of the many hardships we endured. I myself was fortunate in having been shielded from privation, though I witnessed much, and nonetheless suffered devastating losses in my own life. Existence was arduous and tenuous. It does not do to frame my century as idyllic, Kevin. Every citizen was not lain to rest in Elysian Fields. Look at you, my friend. You are young and hale and have health and freedom and enjoy unimaginable luxuries and access to information. You live with the assurance of vaccines and medical procedures that cure or heal all but the most severe ailments, and yet you long for an epoch in which half of all children died before the age of five."

"I know your age was difficult," Kevin said. "I'm not naïve when it comes to anguish. Some people call it the 'good old days,' others believe *these* are the good old days. I think it's relative. After all, health and convenience and abundant leisure are empty if there is no virtue or compassion at an individual's core, if they exist only to serve the *self!*" He heard his voice rising but couldn't stop it. "As dazzling as it may seem, there are major social instabilities at the foundation of twenty-first-century life. We're more connected than ever by way of our own inventions, but the more technology advances, the more disconnected emotionally and spiritually from one another we become. Things are becoming less personal. Style has been replaced with affectation. Hell, they're not even teaching handwriting in schools anymore!"

"There are major social instabilities at the foundations

138

of many societies," Coletta observed. "Perhaps the point is not to rail against what you don't like, but find a way to live amongst it in a way that doesn't compromise your own beliefs."

"The basic breakdown of manners and morals is what I'm referring to. It makes even the smallest interaction frustrating and irritating," Kevin said.

"Right, but it doesn't have to be that way!" Coletta said. "You take everything too personally, as an affront to *your* conception of how people should behave."

Kevin crossed his arms and huffed. "Well, I'm not going to be like them."

The music in the café suddenly cut, and the TV volume went up. The barista was gawping at the screen. Kevin looked at it too. There was a horde of blinding flashing lights clustered at the foot of Link Tower. A disheveled, grieved Roberta Denton stood just beyond a line of police tape. It was a section of Central Square that Kevin and Jane and Coletta had walked through not half an hour ago.

". . . *received confirmation from Still City Police just a few moments ago that the mayor has indeed been gravely injured. Whether or not this injury was accidental or intentional is unclear at this time. Again, Mayor John Prise is being rushed via life flight to St. Frederick's Charity hospital tonight after having suffered some traumatic event, the details of which we have yet to learn here at News Channel 9 . . .*"

Kevin was on his feet without realizing it. He stared at the TV, at the commotion going on less than a quarter of a mile from where he stood, and suddenly all he could think about was his mother. He turned to the girls. Coletta looked stunned; Jane regarded him morosely.

"I'm sorry, I have to go. I'll call you later," he said, glancing at Coletta but averting his eyes from Jane's as he turned and left.

The street was pandemonium. What had minutes earlier been the quintessential picture of holiday cheer had turned to a scene of confusion and panic. Helicopters hovered over Link Tower. A crowd of stunned onlookers, arms loaded with festive shopping bags, had gathered near the perimeter of the area that had been taped off by the police and were gazing into the square where a group of heavily armed guards in protective vests paced like soldiers. Kevin only needed to look at their expressions to gauge the seriousness of what had occurred. A random image flashed in his mind of John drinking beer with Frank in the backyard of the West 9th Street house. They were hysterical, recounting some wild tale from their days as college roommates, John laughing so hard he knocked his bottle over, which proceeded to roll off the table and spill into Frank's lap. "Just like old times," Kevin's father said as he brushed the foamy beer off his shorts. It was the last time they saw each other.

Kevin turned away from the chaos and started down West 11th in the direction of the river. Out here the city was eerily still and silent except for the random emergency vehicle blazing toward Central Square. He made his way down to the embankment, followed the meander of the Kiksuyapi, and crossed the old drawbridge into Dovetree. As he walked, Jane's words echoed in his mind. *Is there no value in now?* The question dominated his thoughts, and though it was anathema to his personal principles, Kevin found himself applying this bit of rhetoric to every aspect of his life: school, his studies, the city, his mother. He thought of his father's rouged face in the coffin, remembered the shadow that had fallen over it as they closed the lid on him forever. *Forever.* For a year after the funeral, he'd dreamed almost nightly of his father opening his eyes at that moment and turning to Kevin, mouth open in a scream as the lid came down. The shadow had spread over Kevin that day as well; in a way, it had buried him alive.

Is there no value in now?

He looked at the façades of the houses he'd grown up personifying as wise and urbane ancestors, stylistic landmarks, cultural progenitors, the core of Still City's identity. *They've been done a wrong,* he'd always thought. But now as he cut through Garfield Park their stares were vacant and cold, their decades of seemingly accumulated wisdom a fable. They were blank and mute and offered no comfort, no guidance or assurance.

Is there no value in now?

He thought of his mother, of his anger toward her because of Chaz and because she'd dared to try to move on from her dead husband. Perhaps she had been asking herself that same question. And did he hate her for answering "yes"? It seemed wholly illogical, and yet he knew that he did, though as the thought evolved, he understood that it wasn't his mother he hated, but the fact that he had been presented with that same conundrum and hadn't the strength to make the right choice—that of Moving On. This made him angry at himself and jealous of his mother's courage. This was the genesis of their emotional isolation from each other, and his isolation from human society in general. His loyalty was to the Dead. How he'd ran to them when they'd beckoned, without hesitation—those he fancied *he* could save and, through them, re-live what had been. But *Then* was gone, and it would not return. Suddenly the essence of Jane's argument came into focus for him; the horror of allowing *Now* to become *Then* with no regard for what should be lived before it is lost. But there was still time, wasn't there? He picked up speed across the footbridge and took the stairs leading up the hill two at a time. As he approached the house, he noticed his mother's car was gone, and Chaz's truck parked at a crazy angle in the driveway. The windows were dark, except for the living room where a single lamp glowed.

Something was wrong. The premonition crept up Kevin's spine like cold fingers. He walked quickly to the front door. As soon as he stepped into the foyer Chaz was there, his face white-gray in the low light. He looked ten years older in that light, all the cool guy swagger gone. The house was silent. Kevin recognized the silence, for it was the same kind that had hung like a shroud in every room after his father's death.

"Where's my mom?" Kevin asked; it came out more

141

as a statement than a question.

"She's was in an accident . . ." Chaz said in a voice flat and soulless as stone, a stone that pressed down on Kevin, with all the weight of the truly Now.

7

"I think that I was too forthright with him," Jane said to Coletta as they left the café. They cut down an alley in an attempt to avoid the chaos, Coletta offering to show Jane the way to Greysworth before heading back to the east side.

"You challenged his entire conception of the world and his place in it. I think that was a good thing. I don't think his belief system gets challenged very often. He's too passionate about it to just cast it aside," Coletta said, then thought: *But that's what I like about him.*

"Yet I fear that my criticism was indelicate. He is kind, and it pains me to think that I have caused his spirit tumult."

"He's strong. I'm sure he'll think about it and take what you said to heart."

They approached the end of the alley. There was a dark gray SUV parked along the curb directly ahead. In the glare of one of the streetlights, Coletta saw the shadow of "PS" on the passenger side door—perhaps a decal that had recently been removed. The door suddenly opened and a man got out. Coletta recognized his scruffy blond hair and black clothes from the coffee shop. He was coming quickly toward them. Coletta stopped, grabbed Jane's arm.

"Come on, let's go back," she said. They turned in unison and saw the other man with the skull cap of black hair, only a few paces in front of them. It happened quickly. The black-haired man elbowed Coletta in the ribs and back-hand slapped her into the wall. She fell to her knees, spitting blood, helpless as she watched the two men approach Jane. Jane's hair was a wild tangle. It looked as though the blond man had tried to grab her by it, but she'd eluded him. The sunglasses had fallen off, disclosing her blazing green eyes. She crouched

142

low; the two men hesitated, glancing at each other uncertainly. Jane was surprisingly fast. She faked one way, then lunged, trying to split the gap between them, but the blond man caught her by the collar of Coletta's coat and yanked her back. The other man grabbed her legs and together they ran for the SUV.

As she watched them speed off, Coletta tried to scream, but all that came out was a shrill wheeze. Pain flared through her, sharp and bright in the dark, and she slumped sideways into unconsciousness.

8

Kevin woke in the chair at his mother's bedside, rubbing his neck as he sat up. Jenna Heartstone had been in a coma since arriving at the hospital, and in the several hours since had been unresponsive. Besides the fractures, contusions, tears, and abrasions, the doctors thought that there might be brain damage, possibly permanent. They had allowed Kevin and Chaz to remain in the room with her, since the consensus was 50/50 that she wouldn't last the night. A sort of numbed calm had come over Kevin at this prognosis; his heart seemed to beat slower and slower, as if it would stop at any moment. It hadn't stopped, though, nor had hers. The monitor chirped along at a largo pace, each blip with the potential to be the last.

Across the room Chaz was snoring, scrunched up on a small couch and using his coat as a pillow. Of course Kevin never would have believed it had he been told earlier that morning that he would need Chaz, perhaps more than anyone he'd ever needed in his life, during those last few hours. Chaz had been firm with the facts of the accident, which Kevin had appreciated. Chaz hugged him close several times during the ride, told him he was there, told Kevin he was going to be there no matter what the outcome. And when Kevin finally did see her—and when his own words came back to him like some malevolent curse *I wish it had been you*—he had turned

143

and cried shamelessly into Chaz's Resurrection Foundations polo, and Chaz had held him, and when it was over they hadn't spoken of it again, and Kevin had been grateful for that.

Kevin rose stiffly and stood, looking down at his mother. He caught the glint of shattered windshield glass in Jenna's hair. It was a cold shimmer, remote as the light of frozen stars. He wanted to hold her hand, kiss her forehead, but did not dare touch her out of some superstitious certainty that his would be the touch of Death. He was, after all, cursed—there was no other explanation for what he was seeing. He turned away, needing to get out of the room for a while. He grabbed his sweatshirt and pulled it on as he stepped out into the hall.

The Critical Care wing of SC General was silent at 2 A.M., a vacuumed sort of silence not unlike the one he'd experienced in the room with the dead at Halloween House. He took the stairs to the first floor and strode through the empty lobby to the vending machines, where he bought two coffees—one for him and one for Chaz. He decided to wander a bit, sipping from one of the scalding cups as he gazed at the innocuous art and rows of empty chairs lining the corridors. A low, disembodied voice paged a doctor over the hospital intercom. There was a TV on in the emergency room waiting area; the sound was off, but the screen was a visual cacophony of images and words. Below a white BREAKING NEWS banner, the main headline read MAYOR PRISE ASSASSINATED AT LINK TOWER. The scrolling bar of text below this offered more details: he had suffered a single gunshot wound to the head and was pronounced dead on arrival at the Peterson Clinic. Police had confirmed that they were "following several leads" though "no specifics were being made public at this time." Kevin felt strangely hollow reading the captions; it was real, but also unreal, much as the last several years had been for him. So distracted was he by this feeling that he didn't at once notice that someone was calling his name. When at last he did look away from the

144

screen, he was shocked to see Coletta staggering toward him, half doubled over with a huge bruise on the left side of her face.

"*Jesus!* What happened?"

"We got attacked. Remember those two guys sitting across from us in the café?" Kevin nodded. "They cornered us in an alley. *They took Jane!*"

"What do you mean, *took* her?"

"They kidnapped her! Threw her in an SUV and sped off."

"Did you get the license number?"

"I was too busy trying to breathe with cracked ribs."

"My God . . . I'm sorry. I mean, I'm so sorry I left."

"I just had an X-ray—they're not actually cracked, just feel like it."

"How'd you get here?"

"Some woman found me and insisted on bringing me here. I told the admissions clerk I was eighteen. I don't need my mother down here freaking out, you know?" Coletta looked at him suddenly, narrowed her eyes. "Why are *you* here?" Kevin told her. She put a hand on his shoulder. "I'll come sit with you if you want," she said softly.

"Thanks, but I can't go back up there right now. It's making me crazy being in that room. I need to get out of here for a while. I need some air or something." Kevin rubbed his eyes. They felt waxy and raw. "What color was the SUV?"

"Dark gray with tinted windows."

Kevin frowned.

"What?" Coletta said.

"That's the same description an eyewitness gave of the one that hit my mom. Was it really new and shiny?"

"Yes! Except for . . . there something I remember about the passenger side door. It was dirty, or faded or . . . *dammit,* what was it?"

"You mean like the paint had chipped off?"

"No," Coletta said, "it was like a shadow or an outline. Wait! I remember. It was logo. Two letters—"

"PS," Kevin said.

Coletta nodded, drawing in and exhaling a shuddering breath. "You know what it means."

"Yes. I know where to find Jane."

*

They rode the elevator to the fifth floor. As they walked down the main Critical Care hall, Coletta said: "How will we get in?"

"My mom's key card," Kevin said. "It'll be in her purse. I just have to somehow get to it."

They approached a pair of isolation doors that led to the ICU. The tired-looking ward clerk seated behind the reception desk was typing something from a chart into a computer glanced up and, recognizing Kevin, pushed the button that buzzed them in. Coletta followed Kevin past the quiet, half-lit rooms of catatonic people and hung back while Kevin entered his mother's room.

Chaz was still asleep. A pad of paper embossed with the hospital's logo and a pen lay on a side table standing beside the room's murmuring heating unit. Kevin scrawled a vague note, "Stepping out for a minute—be back soon," and left it on the table along with coffee he'd bought for Chaz. Then he grabbed his coat from the back of the chair, and this time before leaving, he kissed his mother.

He and Coletta went to the nurse's station. The on-duty nurse was a man in dark blue scrubs and black framed glasses; he looked at Kevin over the tops of these, eyebrows raised.

"I'd like to get something from my mother's purse. Her name's Jenna Heartstone."

"I'm sorry. No one is allowed access to a patient's belongings except for the patient," the nurse said. The phone at the station began to ring shrilly.

146

"But I'm her *son!*"

"Family members included," the nurse said as he grabbed the receiver. His expression changed—he hung up quickly, turned suddenly, and hurried down the hall. Other nurses were running in the same direction toward a single sustained beep. A moment later a Code Blue was called over the hospital loudspeakers.

Kevin looked behind the counter at a small closet with glass panels. He could see the purse within, but a heavy padlock hung from the metal tongues connecting the doors.

"I can see it—it's right there!"

"Get it," Coletta hissed.

"How?"

"Look for the key! I'll keep an eye out."

Kevin hesitated.

"Go on, *do* it!"

Crouching, he went behind the desk, scanning for keys, but didn't see any. He opened a drawer that was full of forms, then another containing blood pressure cuffs. In the center drawer were pens and pill samples and vending machine packages of junk food. He searched through it but came up with nothing.

"It's not here," he said.

"Nobody's coming—keep looking!"

A moment later a team of nurses and doctors appeared around the opposite corner. Kevin ducked, fingers white as they gripped the edge of the desk. He heard Coletta stammering something diversionary, but it didn't matter—the team didn't even glance at them as they sprinted in the direction of the Code Blue. From his vantage point, Kevin saw several single keys hanging from a series of hooks along the right wall under the desk. One was small and bronze and attached to a coiled keychain that resembled an old-fashioned telephone cord. He took it, spun around, stuck it in the lock, and turned. The mechanism popped with a clank. Kevin rose, snatched his mother's purse off the shelf, stuck his hand inside, and felt for her keys. He found them after several seconds—seconds that felt like hours—stuffed the keys in his pocket, then tossed the purse back in the cabinet and reattached the lock.

They walked quickly back through the CC wing to the elevator. Preventative Solutions was only a mile and a half from the hospital. Kevin had never been to his mother's place of work before, but was guessing (hoping) that the key card would access all the main doors. He took it out as they rode to the ground floor. There was blood spatter on the gray plastic surface. A breath hitched in his throat. Coletta looked at him.

"What's wrong?"

"Nothing," Kevin said. He wiped card off on the edge of his father's sweatshirt and stuck the key ring back in his pocket. Suddenly, the momentous weight of what had taken place threatened to overwhelm him. Kevin closed his eyes, steadied himself, managed to suppress his grief. He had to—both for Jane's sake as well as his own—for somehow saving her had become inextricably linked to saving himself.

9

Jane sat handcuffed to a chair in the sterile blackness, stripped of her clothing and sopping from the hose. The chair she was bound to was positioned under a catch drain at the center of the slightly sloping floor. It was more than mere test tubes and beakers and chemical reactions at Preventative Solutions. The lab where Jenna Heartstone had spent her mornings and afternoons the past decade was transformed by night into a theatre of horrors in which the "research" conducted—first on small and medium-sized animals and later on vagrants and unsuspecting drunks, who'd woken from their stupors to situations decidedly more grievous than mere hangovers—was on par with wartime human experimentation crimes.

Three men in full protective body suits and masks had performed several tests on Jane while a fourth man dressed in a black suit observed, asking random questions and always referring to Jane as "it." They'd scorched one of her feet with a blowtorch. They'd extended one of her legs, propped it up at the foot using a vertical brace, and dropped a fifty-pound weight onto her knee. The patella shattered—a sound like crunching gravel. Somehow she was still able to walk. She was made to drink a large glass of something white and chalky that made her stomach taut as a drum. They ran a tube down her throat; they X-rayed her. A large section of skin they'd cut from her right cheek lay in a Petri dish across the room beside the jar of formaldehyde containing her left eye. She hadn't felt it when they'd sliced off the chunk of desiccated flesh, but the removal of the eye had been startlingly painful, as if the nerves of sight were woven into her cognitive functions. Finally, a six-inch needle had been inserted into Jane's left temple and a syringe of grayish green fluid extracted. The fluid had glowed like a gas lamp in fog. After they'd collected this, the four men took it with them and left Jane in the dark. She did not know what sort of death this second one would be, and supposed it didn't matter. These men would study her, learn from her, and could she really be angry with them for it? After all, she would not be here in the first place were it not for them. Indirect as it might have been, they had granted her the opportunity to glimpse the future as well as reunite her with her father, and, most gratifying of all, the fortune of meeting Kevin. Oh, how she regretted their argument—how she wished now that she had confessed her feelings instead of futilely arguing. Her heart was dead and dry, but she no less longed to embrace him, dance with him, to assuage some of those inherent yearnings denied her in life. Alas, there wouldn't be a chance. Even now she felt this miraculous gift of revivification beginning to fade. It was a tingle, not a sense of cold, but rather a fluttering of the nerves, then a long and slow dizzying sensation similar to the feeling when a narcotic begins taking effect. It came and went in spaced waves, and with each passing cycle Jane noticed her consciousness dulling a tiny fraction more. Soon, she supposed, the men would return, and this magnificent window, momentarily uncovered, would be cloaked again, this time forever. Would she be allowed to bring these experiences with her? Would these memories, like those from her former life, accompany her back to that fertile fabric which was neither time nor space?

She started when she heard the click of the door latch. Jane squinted in anticipation of those infernal overhead lights, but they didn't turn on. Then she heard a voice, one she recognized, calling her name in a low whisper.

"I am here!" Jane said.

There was some indistinct chatter, followed by the sound of glass crashing to the floor. A second later the fluorescent lights blazed on, and Jane saw Coletta standing in front of her, mouth agape, a sheen of tears in her glassine blue eyes

"Kevin, stay there," Coletta said weakly.

Kevin, approaching from behind. "Why?"

"Just *stay there!*" Coletta repeated, this time with force. Jane heard his footsteps stop a few feet from her chair.

"Do not weep for me. I am in no pain," Jane said.

"We have to find a way to get you free," Coletta said, examining the handcuffs. Jane could see the genuine concern in the girl's eyes, and she loved her for it. She wondered if Kevin recognized this as well. She hoped so. Souls like Coletta were diamond-rare, adamantine in their devotion.

"I have no key," Jane said.

"Maybe it's somewhere around here," Coletta said.

"No," Jane said, "the man in the black suit has it, and he will be returning soon. I thank you, truly, for coming, but you must not remain here."

"No way. We're not leaving you," Kevin said. He was searching the place for something to use to break the chain. Coletta, searching in her own right, had located the clothes in the trash and was pulling them out. Jane looked down at the cuffs around her hands and had an idea then how to get free. She had considered it as soon as the men had left and knew it would work, though her instinct for self-preservation was strong. She marveled at it, this instinct. It was time, however, to sacrifice what required sacrificing. She could not let these two come to harm because of her.

Narrowing her right hand, Jane began to pull against the cuff. Her flesh held fast for a moment, then slowly began to peel back, falling at last to the ground like a discarded glove. She looked at the hand: gray tendon and muscle like freeze-dried meat. In some areas it had been stripped to the bone. The jagged skin of her wrist gaped like a cuff. She freed her left hand the same way, then rose, arms crossed over her chest as she went to the bin where Coletta was sifting out the clothes.

"May I have my dress?" Jane said softly.

"How did you—" Coletta started, then saw Jane's hands. She wept as she helped Jane dress and reattach the coral necklace. Kevin joined them near one of the long tables lined with pH controllers and chromatography columns and modular bioreactors. He wondered at which table his mother sat and felt a pang when he realized she would probably never sit there again. She had clocked out yesterday, hung her lab coat on a hook or in a locker, and there it would hang like an empty cocoon until PS hired her replacement. *Her remains.* They would be all around him, like his father's. At the gravesite, his mother's side of the stone engraved, completed. Remains. That was what he would be left with at Neil Memorial, at his house, full of them—in a deteriorated neighborhood in a city built atop them. As Jane turned to him, as he got his first glimpse of what they'd done to her, Kevin thought it would break him. It was the ultimate wronging, this violation of a relic from a time no longer reachable. It was the clawed bucket of a wrecking machine crashing through the gingerbread gable of an old house.

"We need to get out of here, *now,*" Coletta said.

Kevin scanned the windowless room. There were three sets of doors, including the ones he and Coletta had come in through. They had found the lab by chance—there were no directional signs or building maps that led to this clandestine place. They had wandered the dim corridors of PS headquarters for forty-five minutes searching for Jane. One thing was for certain: they weren't getting out the same way they came in.

Kevin gestured to a single door on the wall to the right. "Let's try that way."

"That looks like it leads to a closet or some ancillary lab," Coletta said.

"I know, but we can't go back. We might as well try it," Kevin said.

"Their transport vehicle carried me through a dark tunnel directly to that entrance," Jane interjected, pointing to the last set of doors across the room.

"I say we go *that* way," Coletta said. "Sounds like our best chance of cover."

Kevin agreed, but as soon as the door shut behind them, they knew it was a mistake. The passage was vast, cold, and utterly black. That astringent stink like melted plastic was overpowering. Jane's remaining eye was the only light in the disorienting darkness. Kevin couldn't be sure, but he thought that it was increasing in luminosity.

"What is this place?" Coletta said, her voice soft yet echoing.

"I think it's some sort of garage. We should go back," Kevin said. He turned around, hands groping for the door handle, but all his fingers found was the thin seam where the doors met. "There's no knob! It must open electronically!"

"Hopefully it's not like that at the other end," Coletta said.

"We should stay close to one another," Jane said. Kevin felt the cold touch of Jane's arm looping through his, and almost simultaneously the warmth of Coletta's through his other.

They proceeded slowly forward, linked together in the blackness, shoes scraping against the concrete underfoot. Ten minutes passed; they felt like an hour. No one spoke. Kevin began to feel the weight of the day pressing on him again. Two hours of sleep at the hospital hadn't been nearly enough and now, despite his nerves, he found himself drifting off. He wanted to find a niche in one of the margins of this place and nap for a while. Just a little while. His body felt so heavy, too heavy to carry, let alone the girls on his arms. Then it occurred to him that they might actually be carrying *him*.

Then the lights went on, and all Kevin's sleepiness evaporated in an instant. He looked around frantically, squinting as he gauged the space. It was some sort of warehouse, lit by a row of hanging dome lights that ran the length of the long passage. The ceiling was perhaps twenty feet high, exposed girders, unfinished. Industrial. Rows of black barrels stamped "PS" in green capitals lined the walls on either side from floor to ceiling. At the end of the corridor, about seventy-five yards ahead, was a wide steel cargo door. Kevin saw a panel with one red and one green button to the right of it. Behind them, the doors to the lab opened. Standing in the doorway was a man in a black suit, his Vandyke honed to a point.

"Where do you think you're going with my specimen?"

Without thinking, the three ran toward the cargo door. There was shouting, other voices approaching from behind. Kevin focused on the green button right of the door. It was still a good fifty-yard sprint away. Now forty yards. Now thirty. Twenty. Coletta glanced over her shoulder, saw the two men who had attacked her in the alley coming up fast behind. When she looked back again, she saw a dozen or so others coming at them head on. They grabbed Kevin and Coletta easily, though Jane again proved much more elusive. She dodged three men, slipped out of the grip of another, ducked under the legs of two more, and an instant later had preternaturally spanned the distance to the control panel. For a moment everyone froze, stunned by the display of agility, or perhaps, frightened by it.

"Jane! Push the green button!" Kevin said, breaking

the silence. A hand yanked his head back by the hair, and then Vexivus's face was two inches from his own.

"Keep your goddamned mouth shut, kid, or you'll end up looking worse than her."

"Worse than my mother?" Kevin said.

Vexivus glared at him a moment, then seemed to understand. His mouth spread into a hideous rictus. The sudden, jarring sound of the cargo door beginning to rise made them both look up. "Release them, and you may have me," Jane said. Her eye was green fire, her wasted figure so fortified with plecebala fumes it seemed as though she might levitate.

"We already have what we need from *you*," Vexivus said, "and now, two disposables to test it on. The fruition of four years of research. You know, it's no accident, that *thing* standing over there. There are a thousand places in this scab of a city to unload any number of burdens, from bodies to by-products. One day I asked myself: what if the two were combined? We knew through your mother's research that plecebala in its pure form is too potent for living patients. But what about dead ones? And not just the newly dead, but the *long* dead? Could they be brought back? Well, yes, they could. More astonishing still, we theorize that the vapor from such a reanimated body can be used as a vehicle to *contain memory*— so that the entire contents of a single mind might be extracted and preserved and stored in gaseous form. There are many tests still to be run, of course. But it's a fitting bit of circumference, don't you think, that your mother's work will be first tested on her own flesh and blood?"

"I don't believe you. My mother would have never participated in this."

"She was elemental in every aspect," Vexivus said coolly. "The very timely death of her husband proved to be the impetus. The bringing back of loved ones and such . . ."

Kevin closed his eyes. It was fitting indeed, the revelation of his and his mother's mutual need to preserve Frank Heartstone. Did Kevin really believe that she had labored with the intent of resurrecting her husband? No. She wasn't insane like Vexivus. But her *work,* just like Kevin's studies, had become an obsession, a narrow ledge from which they'd hung by their fingernails, dangling over a yawning pit of grief.

"You're depraved," Coletta said.

"Shut her up!" Vexivus snapped. One of the men restraining Coletta wrenched her hair back while the other kneed her in the gut. She pitched forward, heaving. Kevin roared. He managed to yank one of his arms free and gouge his captor's eyes, but in the next moment fell on his side, struck in the head by something heavy. He felt himself being dragged back toward the lab. He tried to see where Coletta was, tried to find Jane, but his eyes couldn't seem to focus. He heard a shrill wail then; the sound grew louder, closer— the sound of sirens. The warehouse filled with shouting, weapons cocking. Kevin was released, laid onto the concrete. He was facing the open garage door—a square of night blazing with the flashes of red and blue as police and emergency cars encircled the building. He saw the red and green buttons of the control panel, and to its left something else green. For a moment he thought he was seeing double, then he focused the single glowing eye, and the hand, like an X-ray, gripping the edge of the door.

"Jane," Kevin said, his voice only a flutter, soft as a breath. The approaching lights blurred. A swarm of people surrounded him, blocking his view. Kevin tried to lift his head, tried to see around the face telling him to "lie still," and then everything went black.

IV.

"Ah! May the red rose live alway . . ."

STEPHEN COLLINS FOSTER

"Remembrance—mighty word."

EMILY DICKINSON

Chaz wasn't aware that Kevin had been admitted to the hospital until a nurse, recognizing the boy's emergency contact as a patient in the very same wing four doors down, informed him. By that point—nearly eight o'clock the next morning—Jenna Heartstone had opened her eyes, though she still wasn't able to speak. Chaz didn't tell her about her son, not right away at least. Kevin had suffered a Grade 2 concussion and was being held for observation for the next twenty-four hours. By the afternoon he'd felt well enough to walk, assisted by Chaz, to his mother's room. Kevin told his mother, now rapidly regaining both her motor as well as communicative functions, what had happened. He told her about John. And he told her that he was sorry; it was the cathartic apology, the one that would begin their healing.

Jenna didn't come home until three weeks after Christmas. During that time Chaz stayed at the house with Kevin, who discovered that the demolitionist had as much experience with bringing back old places as he did tearing them down. They talked about Resurrection Foundations' various projects around the city. They talked about Frank Heartstone and his work. Kevin walked Chaz through the house, exhaustively describing every detail his father had restored, Chaz all the while listening with patient attention.

Coletta called and told Kevin about the fire at Greysworth. Neither of them had heard from Jane. They discussed trying to get into Treestone, figuring she had gone there, but the cemetery was still sealed as the EPA began to rid the grounds of PS's filth.

Preventative Solutions itself had ceased operations nationwide as the federal investigation into Still City's contamination and Serge Vexivus's capital murder trial played out publicly, producing no shortage of scandalous headlines, the most shocking of these being Vexivus's acquittal. Though he was released, and subsequently left Still City for a modest position as chief quality officer at PS headquarters on the west coast, he never worked a day there. A tanker truck carrying, ironically, Plaiscene by-product to an undisclosed illegal site, jackknifed on black ice, its contents covering not only a quarter of a mile of mountainous highway but Serge Vexivus's towncar. The chemical turned out not only to be toxic but highly flammable: the subsequent explosion burned so hot that only the car's frame remained.

Meanwhile, the green shroud that had veiled Still City for half a decade dissolved into the clean blue ether of a new January and did not return. And as the pills ran out, the mental haze of the multitude that had relied on Plaiscene daily for succor and security lifted. Their problems didn't go away, though the restored ability to reason helped in dealing with them properly and thus it could be said, bravely.

After lying in state for two days in the restored lobby of Link Tower—forty-eight hours that saw more than ten thousand observe the open coffin—Still City's mayor and native son was buried in the modest Prise family plot beside his mother and father in a small Latvian Orthodox cemetery on the east side of town.

2

Wednesday, the tenth of January, was the first day of a paralyzing cold front that swept in with the New Year—a high of -3 and a wind chill twenty degrees below that. Classes had been canceled. Chaz told his crews to stay home despite being under contract to gut seven east side houses slated for renovation by the end of the month. The power had flickered several times that evening. It was at times like these, Kevin thought, that working fireplaces proved their worth as more than mere novelties. Chaz tended these in the kitchen/dining room and parlor and worked off battery power on his laptop, sending emails and assessing cost analyses on RF's major project of the coming year: the transformation of the derelict D. K. Jorda crayon factory into a new city charter school.

160

Kevin had spent the majority of the day in his room, even though it was at least thirty degrees cooler upstairs. The cold hovered around the frozen window panes like an aura; the glass itself looked so brittle Kevin thought it might shatter if rapped upon. It wouldn't, of course. It had survived through one hundred and twenty-seven winters, most equally as frigid, and would probably survive one hundred and twenty-seven more. Beyond the antique panes, a fur of hoarfrost clung to the world like an invasive species. Like the world outside in the throes of the deep freeze, a numbness had spread through Kevin during the long day. It was as if the pulse of the world was inexorably slowing. A chill that would never diffuse. A frozen heart in contempt of the summons of spring. For the past two weeks he had tried not to think about Jane, about their argument at the café, about the indignities she had suffered that night in the lab. He tried not to think about her alone, grieving for her father and the others. He tried to tell himself that the dead did not grieve, but the more he tried, the more harrowing and heartrending his thoughts became. There was Jane, huddled in the corner of her dark tomb, motherless and now fatherless, waiting either to fade away or to be found by the EPA men in breathing masks and chemical suits—the only ones who haunted Treestone these days. Would they treat her as shamefully as Vexivus had: as an "opportunity"—a *thing* rather than a sentient being? Kevin had let them do this to her the first time, and decided he couldn't let it happen again.

He put on his heaviest overcoat, two layers of socks, boots, and went downstairs. He found Chaz at the dining-room table on the computer. The room was warm from the fire and amber with taper light, but Chaz's face was illumined coldly by the screen's glow.

"I need a ride," Kevin said.

Chaz looked at Kevin's clothes and frowned. "A ride where?"

"To the east side."

Chaz huffed. He wished he could tell the kid "no,"

161

but he knew he had no authority, and didn't want things to become fractious after their relationship had finally normalized. He rubbed his face, glanced at his screen, and then back at Kevin. "Can you give me five minutes?"

"Sure."

Chaz reached in his pocket, threw Kevin the keys. "Go get her warmed up."

It began snowing lightly as they drove east along the band of salt-streaked highway. The truck cab reeked of cherry air freshener and fumes from the leaky exhaust manifold but was cozy with the heater blower on high, where it stayed during the entire drive. Kevin didn't tell Chaz where they were headed, and Chaz didn't ask—only followed directions as Kevin told him to take exit 178 and merge onto Progress Avenue. As they approached East 67th, Chaz mentioned that he was working on some properties in the area.

"Which block?" Kevin said.

"East Seventy-second."

"Can we park there?"

"What are we up to, bud?" Chaz said, without taking his eyes off the road. Kevin didn't answer. The neighborhood was dark; the power seemed to be off on the street, but in Treestone battery-powered flood lights blazed. The truck turned left down East 72nd, passed the cemetery, and pulled into the driveway of a house gutted to its studs and beams. "Townhouse Row. That's what they're renaming these places, though I don't know who the hell's going to buy them now."

"Speaking of which, I need to borrow your ladder," Kevin said, his eyes ticking in the direction of Treestone.

"I'm sorry. No way," Chaz said, putting the truck in reverse. As they started to back out, Kevin unlocked the door and jumped out.

"Hey!" Chaz shouted, hitting the brakes. Kevin was already crossing the street, running through the blowing snow and freezing wind that he felt already needling through his thick knit cap and gloves. Breathing it was like being thrown into icy water. Chaz caught up with him at the eastern rear

162

corner of the cemetery, looking severely pissed—out of patience, at last.

"Get back in the goddamned truck, Kevin!" Chaz said, swiping for his jacket.

Kevin deftly avoided him. "I'm going in there, with or without your help."

"What if you get arrested? Don't you think your mother has been through enough? Don't you give a shit about her feelings?"

"Of course I do," Kevin said. He was crying now, couldn't believe that he was crying. His voice was rising; he felt himself slipping out of control, but he didn't care. "I *need* to do this, and I'll goddamned freeze to death before I leave *without* doing it."

Chaz was staring at him, stunned. Kevin wasn't sure whether it was the fit or the fact that it was freezing that made him finally relent. In any case, Chaz pulled the truck up along Treestone's rear gate, covered in biohazard signage and No Trespassing warnings. He set his adjustable ladder against one of the walls in an obscure section shadowed by a large evergreen. As Kevin climbed, Chaz said: "How will I know when you're ready to come back?"

Kevin surveyed the cemetery from his vantage point on the eighth rung. "That tree on the far side near Progress. I'll climb that to get out. I won't be long. Wait in the truck—and keep the heat going." Before Chaz could answer, Kevin climbed up the rest of the way and leapt over the fence into Treestone.

It was a strange world that he landed in. Snowflakes like flecks of crystal drifted down through the brilliant artificial light, gathering in delicate piles atop the grave markers and the roofs of the mausoleums and the thick tangles of dead vegetation. The grounds were crisscrossed by silhouettes of the ancient bare trees. The cemetery walls buffeted the wind, and the lights provided a semblance of warmth; combined, these factors made the cemetery seem somewhat cozy despite the temperature. Kevin tromped through the silent stillness toward the Cardinal tomb. The door to it stood half open. He walked to the entrance and peered over the threshold into the blackness.

"Jane?" No response. "It's Kevin," he added softly. He pushed the door open all the way, letting in the garish electric light. The tomb appeared empty. He saw the three bronze coffins lying on the daises. The one in the center and the one to its right were empty, but in the far left lay the judge. The lines of his face remained hard, even as his face was relaxed in death. A gray and oily film, blackening on the extremities, had crept over his flesh. And then there were his eyes—there was something *wrong* with his eyes. They were frosted and scaly, quite dead looking, yet still contained the faintest hint of pale green. Kevin went to him, gripping the edge of the coffin, the chill of the metal palpable through his gloves. As he leaned in the eyes looked at him.

Kevin lunged back, gasping, rapidly exhaling little clouds. Behind him, Jane appeared in the doorway. Backlit by the spotlights, she was a glazed thing, her skin burnished by the cold like porcelain. Her hair, two braided loops, hung neck-level. Half her face—the damaged half—was in shadow. When he thought of her in later years, this memory—this image of her—was always prominent in his recollection, for in that moment she seemed timeless, a supernal thing belonging to no era.

"What's happening to him?" Kevin asked.

"He's failing. We all are."

"'We'? But the fire . . ."

"A few escaped the conflagration. The rest chose to remain."

"To be burned up? Why?"

"Perhaps their devotion to the past was larger than the possibilities of the present. For them cremation was the ultimate release, a guarantee that they could never again return."

Kevin sighed. "I'm sorry to hear it. That really is a tragedy."

164

Jane shook her head slightly. "Still, you do not understand . . ."

"Understand what?" Kevin said.

Jane entered the tomb. As she approached him, the void where her left eye had been came into view. Her remaining eye was only the dullest green now, like a clover in the shade. Jane lifted Kevin's right hand, removed his glove, and interdigitated her stripped fingers through his.

"You dream of phantoms, my friend, while those you love stand all around you in the flesh." Jane closed her hand around Kevin's. He stared at her bones, at the web-like strands of dried tendon connecting them. "Do you see?" she whispered. "Do you *see*, my dearest Kevin?"

The light became lambent through his tears. They were warm, soothing on his benumbed cheeks. "I see," he said.

"Celebrate the beauty that you are, share it, now until the end of this life—for the power of living and all its potential does not cease until that force departs us. Promise me that you will *live* these years, however few or long they might be."

"I promise, Jane." Kevin's eyes drifted to the bronze casket in which Judge Elias J. Cardinal lay, somewhere outside of both life and death. *What are his thoughts?* Kevin wondered.

"You are wondering of your own father," Jane said, "of what you would have said to him had he returned."

"I'd considered that in the beginning," Kevin admitted, "and then I couldn't think of it anymore. I wouldn't let myself."

"You were frightened of the deep wound reopening, of being unable to contain the bleeding."

"I know that I wouldn't have wanted to let him go again."

"Yes," Jane said, looking at her father, "I think you are quite right in that."

Kevin shuddered involuntarily. The cold was

becoming paralyzing, the tingling creeping up his feet and blanching his fingers, turning steadily into numbness. Jane released him slowly.

"You must go."

Kevin didn't want to go, but he found himself nodding as he shivered violently. Jane reached behind her neck, unclasped the coral necklace, and coiled it into Kevin's gloved hand.

"This is for Coletta," she said.

"For protection . . ." Kevin said.

"No," Jane said. She leaned in, pressing her frozen lips for a long moment against his cheek before drawing back again, utterly still in the little house of stone. "Just a pretty thing."

EPILOGUE

Kevin's sophomore year concluded on the last day of May. The summer to come promised to be a busy one. He'd scheduled a few college tours. He'd been hired for the season by Resurrection Foundations as a "property research assistant." Essentially, he went with Chaz to newly acquired houses and buildings and helped assess the historical and antique values of the places and their contents. John Prise had in his will named Kevin and his mother as his sole beneficiaries, leaving them a substantial inheritance that covered the balance of Jenna's medical debt and allowed her to keep the house.

Chaz moved in around the time Jenna found out she was pregnant. Kevin had decided to relocate to his father's study, giving up his old room for the baby due sometime around Christmas. Slowly, he began the task of merging his things with Frank's. Books, papers, collectibles. As father and son had both been hoarders of all things antiquity, there was a lot to be considered, and a lot to be parted with. In the end, Kevin kept only those items that held significance to both of them. He moved Frank's desk—the Thomas Farland that Kevin now used—across the room into a niche beside one of the wall-length bookshelves and arranged his bed horizontally along the bay window. Beyond the panes the azaleas his mother and father planted after buying the house in were in full bloom. Jenna, still in rehab for her right knee and dealing with acute morning sickness, would sometimes come in and sit with Kevin. They had settled into a new tranquility. Sometimes they would talk, other times she would just silently regard the flowers. Gradually, the room lost its tomb-like feel.

Kevin didn't return to Treestone again until late that same spring. He'd asked Coletta to meet him there. They hadn't had any classes together the previous semester, and though he'd talked with her a couple times on the phone during the weeks immediately following the events of

167

December, and saw her occasionally in the hall, they hadn't really spoken. But he was looking forward to seeing her again. He wanted to see her again.

The cemetery had reopened to the public in mid-April after three months of extensive ground cleanup and repair. There were still a number of renovations underway: repairing tombs, repaving of paths, updating the section signs. As the 72 pulled up to its stop, Kevin noticed the main gate and perimeter fences had been repainted, and the great Gothic stone arch sandblasted.

The place was quiet, the light lambent on the graves and the freshly mown grass as it passed through the leafy crowns of the trees. Everything looked so different with the brush and trash cleared away. Kevin saw squirrels scurrying up the oaks and sycamores, honeybees deliriously rolling in the pollen-laden dandelions, a robin bleating its mating song while perched atop the curve of a leaning, illegible headstone. Beneath the song he heard another sound—the gurgle and rush of water nearby. As he made his way toward it, Kevin realized it was the fountain. It had been cleared of rubble and debris, as had the centuried brick walkway encircling it. On one of the benches along the outer perimeter he saw Coletta. She wore a pale blue sleeveless top, midnight blue shorts, sandals. Her hair was pulled back and restrained by a long white ribbon.

"Are you going to come and sit down or just hover there like a ghost?" she called.

Kevin strode a half-circle around the fountain, admiring it as he walked. "It's amazing. I didn't know they were planning this."

"Neither did we. All of a sudden there's all this money going into the neighborhood. Probably has something to do with the national news calling us 'Spill City.'"

"Yeah, probably," Kevin chuckled.

They sat in silence for a moment, watching the water gush out of the urn-shaped fount. It collected in a series of tiered disc-shaped basins, then trickled from them into the reflecting pool below.

"How's your mom?" Coletta asked.

"Getting better. She's always going to have pain, though."

Coletta looked down at her toes. "So will you."

Kevin frowned. "What do you mean?"

"Do you still think about her?"

Kevin threw a glance over his shoulder in the direction of the Cardinal tomb. From this vantage point, he could only glimpse a gable and one of the mausoleum's inverted torches through the ring of newly planted boxwood hedges around the fountain's perimeter. "Sometimes. I mostly dream about her."

"Me too."

"You do?"

Coletta nodded. "She's always really happy. I know that sounds stupid."

"Not at all. She is for me too."

"I wish I'd had the chance to say goodbye. And that I'd been able to meet my grandfather."

They were silent a while, looking at the fountain.

"Do you think everything will just go back to normal now? I mean, do you think that everyone will try to forget what happened?"

"I think they'll try. No one will talk about it, just as no one talked about Preventative Solutions. It's up to us to remember, I suppose," Kevin said. "Oh! Speaking of which . . ."

He reached in his pocket and took out the coral necklace. He'd carefully polished each of the beads, though he'd left the patina on the tarnished gold clasp. To him, it was part of what made it beautiful. Made it matter.

"She *gave* it to you?" Coletta said.

"No, she gave it to *you*," Kevin said as he helped her put it on. It looked beautiful—vital and radiant just like her. As he looked at Coletta, something occurred to him. In that moment, he hadn't been thinking of anything past or future, nothing as imminent and nothing in regret. There was only the fountain gush, the robin song, the delirious stridulations of the insects of spring. There was only this girl, and the gift of having the chance to bear witness to her beauty, her youth, her nascent feelings for him, plainly visible in her eyes. *Is this what it's like, to live in the truly now?* he wondered. If it was, he liked it. His instinct was to guard the moment, store it for later observation, bury it in his memory like a jewel in a lock box. Dull and dark. Instead he decided to seize it, hold it to the light.

He took Coletta's hand, lacing his fingers through hers. She brought her other hand around, gently stroking his forearm.

"Should we get out of here?" Kevin said.

"I thought you'd never ask," she said.

In Memory of:

Peter Browning
Esther Cappella
Patricia Cappella
Diane Dubbert
Marvin "Butch" Evans
Mary Eloise Evans
Artie & Rita Fontes
Anna & Telio Giammarco
Mario Giammarco
Irene, Johnny, & Ramon Robles
Robert Robles
Nick Russell
David Weyer
Lee Weyer
Steven Weyer
Foody and Guano
Regal

Acknowledgements.

This story is a piece of my heart in print. It was written and revised during dark days. The light of Victorian lamps figurative and literal lit my way through them.

Love and gratitude to my family: mom and dad and Bryon & Leslie, brothers & sister (and Wyatt!), nieces & nephews, aunts and uncles, grandparents and other family and friends—here and departed.

Thank you to my colleagues: Christa Carmen, Barry Dejasu, doungjai gam, Curtis M. Lawson, Alison Littlewood, and Clint Smith. We may not see each other often, but I am grateful for your advice, counsel, revision suggestions, and camaraderie. And all the books! I am honored to have the privilege of calling you Friends. Also, thanks to Linda and Grace and all the staff at the Cleveland Public Library - Jefferson Branch for all their kindness and assistance.

Thank you to S. T. Joshi—ever generous with his time and a true lantern in the dark for nascent authors such as myself. This book benefited much from his assiduous edits. And thanks to Amy Brady for her edits, suggestions, and encouragement, and to Mary for the same and for her love and unwavering support.

I had the honor of revising part of this book in Emily Dickinson's bedroom during an "A Mighty Room" studio session. Visit https://www.emilydickinsonmuseum.org/ for more information

About the Author.

Joshua Rex is an author of speculative fiction and historical nonfiction. His debut collection *What's Coming for You* was published in August 2020. He lives in the Midwest, where he is an M.A., History candidate at Bowling Green State University.

www.JoshuaRex.com

Made in the USA
Middletown, DE
13 August 2022

70271769R00104